A HOLIDAY IN BOLOGNA

Heidi Manelli arrives in Italy on a mission. A letter and documents given to her on her 21st birthday revealed that her true family name is Soleari, and she has family living in Bologna. Orphaned, she is unsure how her estranged relatives will receive her. Standing outside the Villa Rosa, she encounters the quietly charismatic yet aloof Stefano. He's suspicious of her sudden appearance and disinclined to believe who she is. After pleading from her cousin Rosa, Heidi reluctantly agrees to stay at the villa, where she swiftly discovers further mystery and danger. She turns to Stefano for help — but will he come through? Is their developing relationship a holiday romance, or something deeper? And is her holiday in Bologna going to change her life forever?

30
1 2£0

LINDSAY TOWNSEND

♦

A HOLIDAY
IN BOLOGNA

Complete and Unabridged

LINFORD
Leicester

First published in Great Britain in 2009

First Linford Edition
published 2023

*A catalogue record for this book is available
from the British Library.*

ISBN 978–1–4448–5005–5

Published by
Ulverscroft Limited
Anstey, Leicestershire

Printed and bound in Great Britain by
TJ Books Ltd., Padstow, Cornwall

This book is printed on acid-free paper

1

Shading her eyes from a stiff breeze and the noon-day sun, Heidi stared through the high metal gates at an elegant stone tower and tiled roof. The rest of the villa was hidden by an avenue of pines, but somewhere within this grand Italian house were members of her family, people whom she had never met or known about until last month.

Standing on the pavement outside this imposing house on a warm, windy day in April, footsore after walking from her hotel in the center of Bologna to this villa on the rising outskirts of the city, Heidi felt her stomach fluttering with anxiety and anticipation. She was tempted to turn away. None of her relations knew who she was, or knew she was coming. She had ventured here out of curiosity, compelled to learn more about her father's family; driven too by a desire to belong, to be accepted by her own flesh and blood.

Her heart beating fast as part of her longed to push open these iron gates, Heidi swung her blue shoulderbag onto the pavement and glanced at the letter in her left hand. A letter handed to her, along with other documents and photographs, by her solicitor, Mr. Weaver, when she called in at his office three weeks ago, on her twenty-first birthday.

'This is from your father,' Mr. Weaver had explained in his dry, rather old-fashioned manner. 'He left it with me in the event of his death, with instructions that you were to receive it on attaining your majority.'

The bulky manila envelope had contained photographs and a letter in her father's familiar untidy scrawl — the letter she had gripped in her hand. She'd read it so often that she could remember everything he'd written.

'*My dear Heidi*,' she murmured, hearing her father's voice in her mind.

'*I must ask for your kindness in this letter, and I hope for your understanding. I'd* wanted to explain in person but must do my best through these poor pages.

'You have always known me as Ruggiero Manelli. That is not my original name, although to me it is my true name, the name I have become known by in my modest career as a photographer. I wanted any success to come as a result of my own efforts and not because of my family's name.

'I had another reason for changing my name, one even more relevant. I loved your mother, Sarah, with all my heart. She was everything to me. My cousin, Federico, never appreciated this, and at the time when we were still talking, seemed to me to make no effort to understand. He and his wife, Rosa, opposed our marriage. They wanted me to stop 'this nonsense' with photography and devote myself to the family business, in which I had no interest or aptitude.

'After many quarrels, I broke with my cousin and was determined to make a new life with Sarah in my newly adopted country. I changed my name as a further severing of any ties.

'I now regret that I broke so completely

3

with my people, but I have never regretted marrying your mother. She made me happier than I had ever known it possible to be happy. Sarah often tried to persuade me to be reconciled with my family, but I suppose I was too proud — I always put it off. After Sarah's death, I could not bear the thought of my elder cousin's pity and so another chance at reconciliation was lost.

'Watching you play at my feet, little Heidi, I realize that I have deprived you of your heritage. Although I had no interest in the family business, you may wish to be involved. You may wish to make yourself known to the family.

'I have enclosed family photographs with this letter and papers proving who I am. Your true family name is not Manelli but Soleari, the name on these documents. Perhaps with you, Heidi, there will be reconciliation. If that is what you want, I pray that it occurs. With all my love, Papa.'

'*Papa,*' Heidi repeated, coming back to the present and her own dilemma. She had chosen to take her first holiday in five years in northern Italy. She

4

had chosen to stay in Bologna where she now knew her family lived and worked. This was their house, the Villa Rosa. She could read the name on the whitewashed stone pillars of the main gate.

Should she make herself known? Should she go on, through the gate?

She had studied this view of these high iron gates before, in one of the photographs her father had left her. One thing the picture had not shown was the scale. The villa was far larger than she'd expected.

'I'll be the poor relation,' Heidi murmured. 'They might think I'm only here for what I can get, for money.' The idea filled her with horror.

Crouching on the hot pavement, her long black hair flicking against her shoulders in the breeze, Heidi dug through her bag with nimble fingers and brought out the old color photograph of her father standing before these gates, smoking a cigarette. *Papa* had never smoked in the time she'd known him. He looked impossibly young, grinning at the camera with his cigarette in one hand and his other arm hugging the shoulders of a pale, slender, dark-haired woman dressed in an elegantly tailored tweed suit and pearls. Not a cousin by blood but a cousin by marriage, perhaps?

With the tip of a finger, Heidi traced the outline of the woman's face. This might be her cousin Rosa. The photograph trembled in her hand as a familiar ache of longing and sadness for her own lost family flooded through her.

'They did send a splendid wreath,' Mr. Weaver had told her, his mouth tight with disapproval, 'but when they made no effort to get in touch, your maternal grandmother concluded that they had no interest in you and never wrote to them again. She decided to say nothing to you to save you disappointment.'

Heidi could understand her grand-mother Christine's reaction. Over the last few weeks she had been disappointed, sad and angry. She had come to this villa in Bologna partly as an act of defiance, to see and then to put her father's family finally behind her. Now that she was so close to their home, it was turning out to be not as easy as she'd imagined.

A sly gust of wind whipped the paper from her other hand and sent it tumbling through the slats of the iron gate and along the driveway.

'No!' Heidi started after the whirling, precious scrap, opening and slipping through the gates before she had even considered what she was doing. 'I'm not losing you, too!' Her reaching fingers closed around her father's letter.

'May I help you?' asked a male voice in English, a few meters off to Heidi's right.

'No, I'm fine, thanks,' said Heidi, rising to face whoever was emerging from the shadows of the pine trees. 'Just a piece of paper. I'm sorry to be a nuisance. I'm going now.'

Her voice trailed away as the man stepped onto the drive. He was smiling and, to her relief, not in the least annoyed at her possible trespass. 'That's quite all right. You don't have to hurry off,' he was saying. 'Are you lost? Would you like directions? Would you like me to call you a taxi?'

He walked past her, his long legs rapid over the flagstones, and opened the gate again to retrieve Heidi's forgotten shoulderbag. 'I believe this is yours also?' he said, holding out the blue bag with another smile.

'Thank you.' Hoping she wasn't staring, Heidi took the bag from him. It was cool standing under the shade of the pine trees, but her face and the back of her neck felt hot. Whoever this man was, he seemed to have no idea of his initial impact on her and for that, she was grateful.

He was handsome in a lean, intelligent, patrician way, and very polite, but clever and charming men were not unknown to her. Perhaps it was the strange and immediate sense she had that he might be important to her, and that there was far more about him than his blond good looks. He was older than her, somewhere in his early thirties, with long, narrow features and eyebrows darker than his wavy, straw-colored hair. Behind steel designer spectacles, a pair of bright brown eyes considered her amiably and frankly enough, though with a certain reserve. Aristocratic detachment? she thought, torn between amusement and exasperation. He was dressed in an old but neat pair of jeans and a navy shirt that set off his tan and carried several cut roses and a pruner. She did not think that he was the gardener.

'Are you lost?' He repeated his earlier question.

'I'm fine, thank you,' Heidi responded crisply. He was still looking at her in that considering way, as if wondering if they had met before. To her irritation she found herself stiffening, her head and shoulders very straight. She was determined not to check on her own appearance, not to fiddle with her long straight hair or her softly styled black silk trousers and loose fitting shell pink top. He made her feel like a nervous job applicant.

Taller than Heidi by almost a foot, he took a step towards her and Heidi's grip tightened on her bag.

'You're on holiday?' he asked. 'Is this your first trip to Bologna?'

'My first trip to Italy,' Heidi answered. 'I like its history and culture. And the food — I love the food,' she went on, smiling herself as his brown eyes gleamed behind their spectacles. When he smiled, this man was easy to talk to. Could he be a second cousin? He was young. It wasn't his fault that Federico or Rosa hadn't tried to contact her. If she made herself known to him now, would he approve of her? Why did she want him to approve of her? Why was she glad they were not closely related?

Irritated by this defensive thought, Heidi sharpened her conversation a little. 'Why did you assume I'm English?'

She half-expected him to shrug, or make a joke about her pale skin, but he answered, 'You look English. Lively and shy together, and perhaps thirsty.' Heidi was still unsure whether to be pleased or aggrieved at his comment. His next state-ment surprised her still more. 'There is a café and *gelateria* a quarter-kilometer from here up the hill.' He pointed out into the sunny street. 'Would you accom-pany me there and join me in a drink and an ice cream? Our Italian ice cream is famous.'

'Thank you, I will,' Heidi replied. So much for aristocratic detachment! This man's initial reserve seemed to be disap-pearing fast.

'Good! I'll slip these flowers into the house and fetch my jacket.'

Heidi nodded and prepared to leave the villa, telling herself that this innocent invitation would give her a breathing space. She would write to the family first, take care of her hotel, and not burst in on them unannounced. Her family had made no effort to get in touch after her father's death. They still might not wish to see her. However painful, she must respect that.

'I'm Heidi.' She extended her right hand, only then realizing that she was

11

still holding the color photograph of her father.

'Stefano.' Long, sinewy fingers brushed against hers and were then abruptly withdrawn. Stefano's dancing eyes were suddenly still.

'What is...?' He sounded bewildered, strands of his blond hair blowing into his eyes and against his spectacles as he stared at the picture she was clutching.

Heidi had never felt more appalled and ashamed. She had done this so badly, so clumsily. 'I'm sorry, I was going to explain.'

Stefano's lean mouth soundlessly formed the word 'Who?' as he raised his head to Heidi's crimsoning face. 'Who are you? What is this? Are you a journalist?'

'No! I'm not here to pry.' Heidi held her ground as he came even closer. 'Can we go to the café you mentioned? I think it will be easier — for both of us — if I tell you as we're walking.'

Becoming more withdrawn again with

every second that passed, Stefano shook his head. 'We talk here,' he said curtly, and placed his cut roses and pruner at the base of one of the pine trees. 'I'm waiting.'

Who was he to order her when this family had never acknowledged her existence? Bitterness surged up in Heidi, and she raised her head to glare at Stefano's annoyingly patrician face. 'Don't you dare presume to judge me.' Hearing footsteps approaching along the flagged driveway closer to the house, the part hidden by the trees, she broke off.

'Stefano, is that you?' called a woman in Italian. 'Have you the roses you said you'd gather for me?'

It was Rosa. Heidi recognized her by her pale skin and straight brown hair, cut in a bob, a style that showed off her pretty, even features. She was as slender as she had been in the photo taken years ago with her brother-in-law and wore a tweed skirt, cashmere jumper and pearls.

As she walked towards them, her low heels drumming on the flagstones,

Stefano lowered his blond head and said urgently to Heidi, 'Put that photograph away. Whoever you are, you will not upset her, understand?' Straightening, he went on in a falsely bright voice in Italian, 'Just bringing your flowers, Mamma. This young English tourist stopped to ask for directions.'

Heidi, who could understand Italian better than she could speak it, was irritated at Stefano's deception but not about to dispute his version of events until he turned to her again and demanded in English, 'How long are you staying in Bologna? Two days, three?'

'I'm on holiday for five weeks,' Heidi said flatly, her blue-green eyes flashing as she saw through his crude hint to leave the city quickly.

'Five weeks? A young woman alone?'

'Who says I'm alone?' Stung, Heidi would have added more, but Rosa, who had just joined them, took in an audible breath beside her.

'Can it be? After all these years of waiting?' Rosa whispered in Italian, her hand groping for and finding Stefano's shielding arm. 'Stefano —' Her fingers plucked at his wrist. 'She wears grandmother's earrings!'

She turned paler still as Heidi stared at her in astonishment. Heidi knew that she looked nothing like her father, Ruggiero, but the news that her favorite pearl drop earrings were family heirlooms was a surprise.

'I didn't know,' she stammered in faltering Italian. 'I'd never have worn them today, given you such a shock . . .'

Her cousin Rosa — surely it could be no other — waved aside her apologies. She was recovering color in her thin, elegant features and now she stood away from the hovering Stefano, her eyes taking in Heidi from head to foot.

'You're small and dark, like grandfather,' she announced in English. 'You have his eyes.' She shook her head. 'I can hardly believe it. Federico will be so pleased. You will stay a while? You will have dinner with us and meet the rest of the family? We have so much to talk about, so many changes —'

'Mamma, you must not over-tire or over-excite yourself,' Stefano broke in. Bending to retrieve the pale pink roses at the base of the nearby pine, he handed one to Rosa, his eyes softening as she took it, although his narrow, aristocratic-looking face remained expressionless and aloof.

His eyes narrowed as he turned to Heidi. 'Why did you not say at once who you were?'

Because I hadn't yet made up my mind whether I want to know this family, Heidi almost snapped back, but conscious of Rosa standing next to her, her slender, delicate frame as taut as a harp string, she answered mildly, 'I thought that a bald announcement might be tactless. I know that my father, Ruggiero, was away from Italy and this city for many years.'

A sigh escaped Rosa's lips, but she said nothing. Stefano threw Heidi another glowering look, removing his spectacles and vigorously polishing the lenses as he did so. 'You'd better come inside,' he told her grudgingly, hiding his expressive eyes behind their steel frames as he, Rosa and Heidi began to walk along the driveway towards the family villa.

2

'Do you like this?' Rosa asked Heidi anxiously as the housekeeper-cook placed a plate of zuccotto in front of her. Whenever the courses changed, Rosa had asked her the same question throughout the long dinner. Heidi smiled as she had done before, thanking the departing housekeeper and saying to her cousin, 'Yes, indeed, very much.'

Conscious of Stefano watching her across the circular table, she waited until the other family members had picked up their silver spoons before doing the same. Every dish she had been given was delicious, but she found it hard to swallow and harder to relax. She felt on view and on trial, and she had so many questions for this family. Why had they never tried to contact her?

Nervous and a little resentful, Heidi covered her confusion by taking a sip of wine, glancing under lowered eyelids around the tiled, high-roofed dining room. With its softly gleaming terracotta walls and antique wall lights, its tastefully laid circular table loaded with fine china and Venetian glass on a beautiful, white cut-work tablecloth — Rosa's own work — the dining room was like the rest of the villa Rosa and Stefano had shown her — rich and well-bred.

Very much like the room's occupants, Heidi thought, glancing at the seated figures round the table. She had been introduced and knew their names now; their characters remained elusive.

She smiled at Rosa, sitting beside her, who wasn't eating her zuccotto either. Rosa was nervously plucking at her napkin with one hand and using her other hand to fan herself ineffectually. Studying the older woman's flushed complexion, tired eyes and drooping posture, Heidi was reminded of two of her regular clients and wondered if Rosa was affected in the same way. At around her mid-fifties, her cousin was old enough to be going through the menopause and her health might be suffering.

I can help you, Heidi thought, giving Rosa an encouraging nod before passing onto the family member sitting beside her — not the aloof Stefano, but an older man, small and stocky with curly gray hair, a pink rose buttonhole in his dark suit and a tie that was slightly askew round his neck. This was Federico, her father's older cousin.

He raised his glass to her. 'This wine is the finest moscato, opened specially to celebrate your homecoming!' he said in his gruff Bolognese Italian that reminded Heidi sharply of her father Ruggiero.

Federico, with his rolling sailor's walk and cheerful manner, had been a surprise. She kept puzzling through the meal how it was that he and her father had quarrelled so badly, although it was plain that Federico had a temper. When Rosa dropped in quietly, 'English, Federico,' her husband stiffened, one hand curling threateningly around the slender stem of a wine glass.

As there had been throughout this

careful dinner, an awkward silence fell, this one broken by a new and not altogether sincere voice.

'Oh, I think our country girl understands us, Mamma,' observed the auburn-haired young woman beside Federico, in perfect English. 'Whatever you and Stefano have told her, I think she appreciates who we are.'

As she spoke, Artemisia touched the diamond choker around her neck, smiling at Heidi while trying to catch Stefano's eye across the table.

Heidi refused to be intimidated by her opulent good looks or her expensive designer gown or jewels. 'Yes, I do, Artemisia,' she replied swiftly in her rarely-used Italian.

Artemisia laughed, trying and failing again to catch Stefano's attention. Finishing his zuccotto, Stefano, who had been mostly silent, asked in English, 'Do you still keep the farm?'

'No, that's gone to another relative who has a real feel for the land.' Heidi was surprised that Stefano knew about her maternal grandparents. He must have asked Federico or Rosa about her. 'Farming has to be a vocation in Britain. Although I loved the life, I have my own vocation,' she went on, adding before Stefano could interrogate her about that, 'as an aromatherapist.'

'Massaging men with oils?' Stefano asked with raised eyebrows. Beside Federico, Artemisia sat up, smoothing the flowing sleeves of the black and purple gown into a more elegant line and looking as if someone had dropped a shower of gold into her lap.

'Caring for men and women with chronic conditions such as arthritis, depression, eczema, migraine, stress, even bereavement,' Heidi countered. She had not expected such a crude misconception from Stefano, she'd thought him more intelligent. 'My clients are patients who have drawn as much as they can from conventional medicine. I can help them, too.'

Stefano gave a brief nod. 'My mistake.' His tanned, lean face remained impassive, and he seemed to be still staring down his long aristocratic nose at her, but his eyes registered apology and, to Heidi's surprise, a certain shame.

Artemisia knew no such self-consciousness or restraint. 'What a pity Marco isn't here!' she crowed, her perfectly made-up face glowing with malice. She helped herself to the last of the moscato. 'He adores anything alternative, especially when it involves a woman's touch.'

'Touch is important,' Heidi said steadily, 'and sensitivity.' To her inward triumph, she saw the woman's sultry black eyes flicker and knew that Artemisia had understood her full meaning. As had Stefano, who raised his eyebrows again.

'How long does it take to become an aromatherapist?' he asked.

'I'd say I'm still learning,' Heidi answered, glancing at her untouched plate of zuccotto. 'I suppose it's the same with your business. I understand you have a bakery and bread shop in

Bologna. I looked for it today.'

'Soleari's isn't a just a bakery. It's not a 'bread shop', as you put it,' snapped Artemisia, her pretty mouth turning down at the corners. 'That's like calling a painting by Botticelli a daub.'

'No, we are artists in bread.' Federico wagged a playful finger at Heidi for her apparent blunder. 'The creation of the staff of life, of beautiful bread and pasta, that's our passion. Stefano will tell you it's a serious matter.'

'Touch and sensitivity are important to us, too,' Stefano said with surprising lightness, a smile hovering in his brown eyes. 'But you're right about us always learning.'

'Not everyone can learn,' said Artemisia, giving Heidi a spiteful glare.

'I'd like to see Soleari's sometime,' said Heidi, wondering what to call the business, if not a bread shop. A confectioners?

'It will be my pleasure to be your guide there,' said Stefano, turning so swiftly in his seat to face his father that Heidi wasn't certain if he was mocking her or being sincere.

'Where is Marco?' he asked, in a harsher voice. 'He was supposed to be here tonight so that we could discuss the latest packaging designs.'

Marco, the younger brother, Heidi reminded herself, glancing at a gap in the table settings where Marco would have been sitting, had he been present.

'Relax, big brother, Marco will have it under control,' Artemisia said, checking her reflection in the back of a spoon. 'You know he's a superb designer. Wonderful eye and taste.'

Stefano became if possible even more still than he'd been for most of the meal. 'Where is he?' he repeated. 'Living up to his playboy image in Milan?'

With a scrape of her chair on the floor tiles, Rosa stood up abruptly. 'We'll take coffee in the sitting room,' she announced, nervously wringing her napkin between her hands. 'Heidi, if you've finished your dessert, would you like me to show you to your room?'

'What?' said Heidi and Stefano together, Heidi further distracted by Artemisia's throaty chuckle.

Rosa seemed to shrivel on the spot, but Federico looked up from the dining table's central arrangement of roses and said with blithe unconcern, 'I phoned your hotel and cancelled your room. They know me there, so it was no problem and no charge. Our gardener's gone to fetch your bags.' Federico bowed his curly head to inhale the scent of his rose buttonhole. 'You're staying with us, Heidi, your family, as is only right.'

This was too much. Resentment at the family's arrogance boiled in Heidi. 'You presume to know my plans, Mr. Soleari,' she said, leaving her zuccotto untouched and also rising to her feet. 'But that is not convenient.'

'Doesn't she look just like Ruggiero when she's annoyed?' Federico chuckled, appealing to the stricken Rosa.

'I think, Father, that Heidi is surprised, and with good reason.' Stefano walked around the table and drew back

Heidi's chair. 'Please allow me to escort you to your hotel,' he said. 'I can help sort out this misunderstanding.'

'I don't need your help, thank you,' said Heidi.

'Please —'

'But she's family!' Federico broke into whatever Stefano was going to say, flinging his arms wide.

'Then why have I never heard from you before?' Heidi demanded. She was going to walk out of this house in a few moments, and in her present mood of angry disappointment, she felt she had nothing to lose. 'My *English* grandmother wrote to you, and you didn't even reply. When my father died, none of you came to pay your respects.'

'There were reasons for that.' Suddenly Federico was no longer smiling. His shoulders slumped, and he looked much older. His reaching hand found one of his wife's, while Stefano stared at his parents as if seeing them for the first time and Artemisia leaned back in her chair with apparent casualness.

'It was my fault,' said Rosa, speaking to Heidi but with her eyes fixed on the cut-work tablecloth. 'I was ill for all of that year when we heard of Ruggiero's death.' She took a deep breath. 'I was in hospital being treated for a badly broken leg when we received your grandmother's letter. I'd fallen off a chair while dusting one of these wall lights. I was too ill and in too much pain to come, and Federico didn't want to leave me. But we did write back!'

Heidi shook her head. 'Grandmother told me she'd never had an answer.'

'We wrote,' said Federico bluntly. 'I wrote. When I learned about you, I wrote at once. I could not believe Ruggerio would not tell me this.'

'Why should he?' Heidi answered, flaring up again. 'You made no secret of disapproving of my mother, of his choice.'

'We thought you and your family wanted nothing to do with us,' Rosa whimpered. 'Ruggiero had been so implacable before, so stubborn. Whenever Federico tried to phone him — and he did several times over several years — your father or grandmother always put the phone down on him.'

This was news to Heidi, but she understood *Papa's* reason. 'My father wanted an apology. My grandmother would, too. It was her daughter you disliked.'

'Not disliked,' Rosa pleaded.

Federico went red in the face. 'A man never says sorry!'

Heidi folded her arms and looked Federico in the eye. 'Then he should.'

A brief silence fell.

'I was bull-headed,' Federico admitted bleakly. 'I should have told him that we didn't care who he married, so long as he was happy, but by then neither one of us would willingly speak to the other.'

'Such a waste!' Pale again, Rosa sank back into her chair, raising despairing eyes to each of her family in turn while Federico patted her hand.

Fingers pressed lightly against her shoulder made Heidi start. She turned and found herself staring at Stefano's

29

chest, raised her head and heard him say softly, 'I can still drive you to your hotel, if you wish. This must have been a terrific shock for you.'

'Rosa,' Heidi murmured, feeling dazed by the swiftness of these revelations. Two cousins' stubborn quarrel and a simple misdirected letter had led to years of misunderstandings. It was both terrible and absurd.

'My sister will look after our parents,' said Stefano, still in that gentle voice. 'Let me see you safely back. You've gone whiter than our best flour.'

'I'd like to stay,' Heidi heard herself say. 'That is, if I'm still welcome.'

With a cry, Rosa broke free of her chair and cast herself at Heidi, who swiftly gathered the taller, sobbing figure into her arms.

'I'd love to stay,' she amended, feeling the prick of tears in her own eyes. 'I'd love to.'

3

Stefano took another sip of his strong, bitter coffee and leaned against the jamb of the open kitchen door, staring out over the city rooftops. Closer in the garden were early foraging birds, and from farther off, the distant sound of a dust cart finishing off a night-time collection. The morning dew was burned off, but he had seen it settle, having been up through most of the night, supervising the first baking at the shop.

He stretched and rolled his shoulders. Over the years as a baker, he'd discovered he needed little sleep. He loved these post-dawn hours, when the rest of the family was asleep and the housekeeper-cook had not yet appeared. This was his thinking time, his time, when the villa was quiet, to prepare the family's own bread.

Stefano turned back from the open door and strode across the tiled floor to the large oak kitchen table. Making bread at home was always a pleasure, when he would try to devise new breads or pastas. This morning however, he was not himself. He was on edge, nervous about his proposed changes to the shop-come-bakery that he felt were necessary but which Artemisia and Marco opposed. And when was the last time either of them were up before dawn to fire up the bread-ovens? he thought, with a spurt of mingled amusement and resentment. They wanted the kudos of the business and the money rising from it, but neither wanted the work. That didn't matter to Stefano, but the way that his sister and brother voted at the twice-yearly family board meetings was vital. There would be another meeting at the end of this month, when difficult decisions would have to be made. Soleari's couldn't go on as it was.

Conscious of a lurking tension headache, Stefano had chosen to make a traditional bread that morning, the regional specialty of golden rolls made of *pasta dura* — literally 'tough dough' — that produced a dense, wheaty bread. Made with lard and olive oil, it was an extremely firm dough to work. He'd used his hands and a rolling pin to bind the stiff dough together, and now after rising, it was ready for his next attack. He tipped the dough onto the floured oak boards and began the next stage, trying to release his tensions through the highly physical, satisfying act of kneading.

Stefano frowned as his palms and fingers pounded and pinched. No doubt their newest family member would be able to soothe his headache away with some fragrant oil, but Heidi seemed intent on avoiding him.

Or was he being unfair? In the three days that Heidi had stayed with the family, she had put herself at Rosa's and Federico's disposal. She had been shown round the villa and gardens by Rosa, been told dozens of family anecdotes by Federico, and pored over old photograph albums with both. She seemed eager to know about her family and keen to be pleased by them, so why was he now wary of her? Meeting her outside the garden gate, before he'd known who she was, he'd been tremendously attracted to her. She'd seemed to like him well enough, then.

'So why doesn't she seek me out?' Stefano muttered, deftly dividing the kneaded dough. 'We are not too closely related: we could have a relationship, so why not?' *She could ask the same of you*, an unwelcome inner voice reminded him. He was thirty-two, altogether too old to be afflicted by shyness. 'She's so self-contained,' he murmured. He was impressed, too, by her success in her chosen profession and touched by her losses. Both her parents had died before her tenth birthday, and her maternal grandparents had died when she was nineteen. Heidi was alone in the world, as he had once been, before he was adopted. He understood what that felt like. But what would she think of him, once she knew he was adopted? Would she be wary of him, a man with no kin of his own to acknowledge him?

Heidi. Stefano found himself smiling as he pictured her, small and slim, with black hair spilling down her back and understanding blue-green eyes. She had a tiny gap between her front teeth that she was self-conscious about. She laughed often, as in spite of herself, but when she smiled, she rarely showed her teeth. He found that endearing. He wanted to know her better, an interest he'd rarely felt since the tragic death of his fiancée, Giulietta; killed by a hit-and-run motorcyclist five years ago, when she was just twenty-one.

Had Heidi anyone special waiting for her at home? At the thought, Stefano's fingers were stilled. He hoped she was free. He hoped that whenever Marco returned from wherever and whatever he was doing, that Heidi would be immune to his younger brother's easy charm and good looks. And of course he would need to tell her of his adoption.

Scowling, Stefano laid the last of the rolls onto the baking sheet and placed the rolls in a cool oven for a few minutes. As he took them out again and set them under a new cloth for their second rise, he had a sense of someone watching and turned towards the door leading to the main house.

Heidi came into the kitchen. 'You're an early riser, too. I was hoping you were. I've an idea I'd like to run past you.'

'Would you like some coffee?' Trying to hide his surprise, Stefano nodded to the espresso machine close to the sink. 'Or tea?'

★ ★ ★

'Tea, please,' Heidi answered, wondering if she should make it but unsure whether Stefano would consider that an impertinence. She had been watching him from the doorway, finding herself almost mesmerized by his clean, long-fingered nimble hands as they effortlessly shaped and molded the unyielding bread dough. For an instant she imagined the touch of those hands and felt herself blushing.

'Your room is comfortable?' Stefano asked, producing a small china teapot from one of the kitchen cupboards and setting the kettle to boil.

'Yes, thank you.' The villa, with its many beautifully tiled and wood paneled rooms and elegant furnishings, was far more exotic than her modest hotel room would have been. As she thought of that, Heidi decided to admit something else, which for some reason had been troubling her.

'I didn't plan to come to Italy alone, you know,' she said quickly, 'but Monica — she's my best friend who was going to come with me — got glandular fever less than a week before we were due to fly out and was far too poorly to travel. I'd arranged for my regular clients to be seen by another aromatherapist and it wouldn't have been fair on her or my patients if I'd suddenly cancelled. This is the first holiday I've had in five years.'

'You were coming with a girlfriend?'

'Yes.' Meeting his eyes, Heidi wondered if he still disapproved, but then he smiled, holding aloft a tray of tea.

'Where would you like to drink this?' he asked.

They sat at the kitchen table, close to the rising bread rolls, Heidi with a mug of tea and Stefano with another coffee. He'd told her how he'd always been fascinated by the magic of bread, the way it changed, its wonderful smell, texture and taste. Heidi was glad of this more approachable Stefano, and she recalled too how considerate he'd been on the night Federico had cancelled her hotel room, offering to drive her back and to help her.

'What is it you want to run by me?'

Stefano's question interrupted her reverie and returned Heidi to another of her more pressing concerns. 'That seems to be a phrase I've heard a lot over these past few days: 'Ask Stefano',' she said, making a small joke. 'So I'm asking. I think your mother would benefit from a course of aromatherapy, and I'd be very happy to treat her, free of charge, while I'm here. I always carry a small batch of oils with me, for my own use. They really do work, you know. So how would you feel about that?'

Stefano raised thick blond eyebrows. 'You think I'd be resistant to the idea?'

'Well, maybe,' Heidi said. 'But I think I can help your mother, and that's all that matters, isn't it?'

She saw his eyes soften behind his forbidding steel spectacle frames, but his answer was interrupted.

'If you're offering free trials, cousin, why not attend my fashion party this morning in our music room? The housekeeper and her husband are going to move the piano out of the way and bring in chairs — just a few. This is a select party.' Artemisia, in a black silk kimono, her auburn hair artfully tousled, paused in the doorway before continuing into the kitchen. 'Won't those rolls be ready to go in?' she teased, ignoring Stefano's taut response of 'Don't tell me how to bake,' as she homed in on the espresso machine.

'You could do a talk and demonstration in the use of essential oils for us,'

Artemisia went on, helping herself to a demitasse of coffee. 'Mother will be there, hovering ineffectually in the background as always.'

'Artemisia, that's uncalled for and unfair.'

The redhead shrugged off her brother's remark, leaning against the sink as she studied Heidi with glinting malicious eyes. 'It will bring the gathering to a nice little close. The Contessa is always appreciative of light relief.'

Any more put-downs you can work in, Artemisia? thought Heidi, amused. 'I'll be very happy to give a demonstration.'

'I won't expect you to buy anything,' Artemisia drawled. 'The designs are very expensive, exclusive.'

'That's all you care about, isn't it?' Stefano broke in, his lean, handsome face rigid in frozen distaste. 'Exclusivity. Selectivity.'

With a casual, unconscious skill, he opened the wood-burning oven, checked the heat with his hand and placed the bread inside, his movements stiff but still agile and strangely graceful to Heidi.

'Excuse me.' He addressed her, his eyes meeting hers for a moment before he strode through the open kitchen door into the terraced garden.

'He'll be back to fuss over the bread.' Artemisia yawned, showing even teeth. 'I'd lend you a dress to wear this morning, but you're so skinny I don't have anything that would fit. Shall I translate at your demonstration for you?'

'No thanks.' Heidi shook her head, only too well aware of how her reluctant relative might twist her words. 'I'm sure the Contessa and your other guests will understand me perfectly. After all, English is the international language.'

Rising from the table, she too left the room, returning to the kitchen only when Rosa called her down from her bedroom to say that breakfast was ready and would she like tea or coffee with her fresh morning rolls?

★ ★ ★

Afterwards, Heidi felt that her talk to the Contessa and the other society ladies after their fashion show had gone well. She was used to explaining and demonstrating the benefits of aromatherapy, with its healing essential oils — the beautifully perfumed and powerful essence of plants and flowers such as rose and lavender, and resins such as frankincense — obtained by steam distillation. Even Artemisia's slightly off-color asides about the uses of oils in 'sensual' massage with a male partner did not put her off.

Halfway through her talk, the door to the music room opened and Stefano slipped inside to stand beside the harp at the back of the room. At the sight of him, Heidi felt her spirits unaccountably lifting, especially when she told her final story about lavender oil.

'This oil is a staple for aromatherapists,' she explained, passing round a small perfume stick of the oil for the listening women to inhale. 'It once saved Mr. Gattefossé, the French chemist who gave us the word aromatherapy, from the effects of a really bad burn. There was an accident in his lab where he burned his hand. He plunged his hand into the nearest liquid that happened to be a vat of lavender oil and discovered that the pain stopped immediately. Further experiments with lavender and other essential oils proved to Mr. Gattefossé that they accelerated healing. This is true not only of burns but of many other conditions.'

From the corner of her eye, Heidi saw Stefano straighten and unfold his arms and knew that she had convinced him. A glance at Rosa, sitting in the shadow of a huge arrangement of white roses, showed her looking interested and also — Heidi was sure of this — cautiously optimistic.

Feeling progress had been made, Heidi decided to leave it another day before she tentatively broached the possibility of treating Rosa. As she packed away her things, several of the fashion-party guests, including the Contessa, asked if she was coming with them to lunch at Notai, one of Bologna's more exclusive restaurants with its famous Art Nouveau décor. Heidi politely put them off, sure that Artemisia would not welcome her. As her talk had progressed, Artemisia, sitting on the front row, looked increasingly sulky.

Soon only she and Stefano were left in the room, Stefano moved the grand piano back to its place with an ease that told Heidi a great deal about his lean, rangy strength.

'That was fascinating,' he said, lifting the piano lid and trying a soft top A with his thumb. 'Thank you. I think Mamma especially really enjoyed it. Have you any plans for the rest of today? Lunch, for instance?'

'None that I know of,' Heidi said, her heart quickening as Stefano left the piano and walked towards her. His face was grave, but his eyes were warm.

'Would you have lunch with me? At Soleari's?' He lowered his blond head to her. 'I'd like to fulfil my earlier promise and show you 'round. You did say you loved food.'

'I do, especially bread,' Heidi admitted, glancing down at herself as Stefano's expression became quizzical. 'I know it doesn't show. I'm as skinny as a pin.' Her grandfather's nickname for her had been String-bean.

'I'd say slender.'

'Whatever.' Heidi smiled up at him, happy that he'd remembered his promise. Intrigued and excited, she nodded at her small carrying case of oils. 'I'll put this away and fetch my bag.'

4

Outside the villa, Stefano asked, 'Do we walk or drive?'

'Walk for me, please.'

'That's not like my sister or mother,' her companion grunted, opening the iron gate for her.

Heidi took advantage of the mention of Rosa. 'Stefano, I don't know how to put this without seeming to be intrusive, but I'm going to say it anyway. Rosa appears anxious, too anxious. You're very protective of her, and that's good, but does she need other help?'

'Medical help, do you mean?' Stefano picked up as Heidi faltered. 'I know she's seen our family doctor. When I asked her about it she told me, 'Only women's troubles,' but I think there's more. I know she's worried about the business. I think there's something about my father, too. I'm not sure what.'

They were out in the street by now,

walking down the hill towards the city. Students milled round them, carrying armloads of books, and from across the road a middle-aged woman carrying a basket loaded with glossy purple aubergines called out a greeting. Stefano waved, saying softly to Heidi, 'One of Soleari's regulars. She'll be asking me about you tomorrow in the shop.'

Heidi smiled at the thought, then nervously checked the position of her shoulderbag as she wondered how Stefano would answer that question. 'Is your father not well?' she asked, returning to their earlier discussion.

'No, no, he's as strong as a horse. He's virtually retired and delighted to be so.'

'Glad to be out of the kitchen?'

'Yes, possibly.' Stefano nodded at another passing customer. 'With any other Italian man I might have thought 'other woman,' but I can't see that with my father. He's devoted to my mother. He even renamed the villa after her.'

I wonder if Rosa sees it that way. Heidi thought, saying aloud, 'Well, whatever's troubling your mother, I'll do my best to help if she's agreeable to my treating her. And if she chooses to tell me anything during her aromatherapy sessions, I promise you now that it won't go further. Our talks will be confidential. That's part of the therapist's professional code of conduct.'

'Like the confessional?' Stefano's somber face broke into a smile. 'Perhaps that's just what Mamma needs. She was very intrigued by your talk, I could tell.'

'That's good,' Heidi agreed, her spirits lifting further as she mentally began to match possible treatments and oils to Rosa.

Meanwhile she and Stefano had begun threading their way through a jumble of medieval and Renaissance streets towards the heart of Bologna, the city of arcades and fresh pasta shops selling world-famous tortellini, the site of the oldest university in western Europe and still a place of culture and politics. Heidi saw several left-wing political slogans daubed on walls between the bookshops and posters announcing the forthcoming opera season. She wondered what it must be like to be brought up in such a bustling, thriving place and envied Stefano, who kept glancing her way, checking that she was not tiring, that there were no mopeds roaring up behind them through the arcades. Conscious of her shoe heels on the stone flags, she turned with him into one of the many squares in the city, close to the food market and the two massive, steepling military towers that loomed over the old center of Bologna, relics of the city's more violent past.

She and Stefano crossed the square, passing some workmen who were snatching a break from their drilling, smoking cigarettes and discussing something with animated hand gestures. Heidi found she could understand their rasping speech. 'So who *are* better at football — Italians or Brazilians?' one was saying, punching the air with a fist for emphasis.

'Football's close to a religion here,' said Stefano with a small grin. 'Not far now,' he added, his face taking on a look which Heidi could only describe as excited anticipation. She found his enthusiasm endearing. She was equally enthusiastic about aromatherapy.

They rounded a corner into another small square, Stefano's stride lengthening as they closed on an arcade draped in heavy purple awnings that would be drawn down in summer to shade the customers and visitors.

'Hi, Stefano!' called the barber from inside his shop.

'Good day, signore,' said the florist, coming to stand in the doorway as Stefano and Heidi wandered past.

Stefano acknowledged both greetings and waved at one of the waiters hovering under the gaudy umbrellas of the café opposite. 'That's Luigi's. They serve wonderful coffee and they buy a lot of our cakes. Very good customers,' he explained softly to Heidi, now pointing to the gleaming shop front just a few paces ahead of them. A hand-painted sign over the doorway read 'Soleari's' in curving gold script. 'Here we are,' he said, opening the door for her.

'Goodness me!' The exclamation burst from Heidi before she could even think to contain it, not that she wanted to. The large shop window, its frame painted a dark umber, contained a magnificent display, different from anything she had seen in Britain. In undisguised delight, she stared at the be-ribboned bags of pasta and breadsticks displayed on brightly painted red, white and green racks. There were cakes on tiers, rich with fruit and dark with spices, and trays of savory vol-au-vents and other delicacies. Beside each kind of fresh pasta was a descriptive tag, written in a copperplate script. Staring at a packet of tortellini, Heidi translated the Italian in her own head, 'Navels of Venus–for lovers,' — and felt herself blushing. Quickly, she glanced at the rising glass shelves in the middle of the window display, where Soleari's famous breads were laid out to admire: flat loaves, plaits and little rolls made in the traditional Bolognese shapes.

'We call that a *crocetta*,' Stefano explained beside her, pointing to a crusty X shaped cross of bread.

Heidi stared at the various sizes of *crocetta*. 'That one's tiny.' Her fingers briefly touched the window glass as she pointed to the smallest cross.

Stefano grinned. 'That's a *ragnino*, a little spider. How did you get into aromatherapy?' he asked, glancing at her hand.

'I suppose because of my grandfather.' Heidi reluctantly tore her eyes away from the ribbons of the window display. 'Farming can be a tough life. Granddad suffered almost continually from backache and none of the conventional medical treatments worked for long. I read an article about aromatherapy and its uses in treating that kind of chronic pain and thought it was worth looking into. I started from there, really.'

She stopped, not wanting to admit that she'd been drawn to aromatherapy for other, possibly frivolous reasons.

The scents and simple beauty of the oils had attracted her. 'It was very hard work on the farm,' she murmured. 'I'd have liked to make bread, but there was so little time.' The farm had taken all of her grandparents' and, as she grew up, her own energies. The aromatherapy, quite apart from helping her grandfather and later, when she'd begun to form her own client base, bringing in welcome spare money to the farm, had given her a break from a largely utilitarian existence.

Maybe that's why I feel so much at home here, Heidi thought, giving the bright, pretty window display another glance. *On our farm we were largely starved of beauty, because the living was so hard.*

'You're welcome to try your hand at baking while you're here. It would be my pleasure to teach you.' Stefano took her hand in his, the first time he had touched her, and added, in a deliberately lighter tone, 'Shall we go in before the staff and customers crick their necks with curiosity?' He guided her inside.

Even ahead of the wonderful scent of

freshly baked bread, the number of customers struck Heidi. There was over a dozen people crowded inside this long, narrow shop, calling out orders to the three employees. At the very back of the shop were two huge brick-built bread ovens. 'The engine room,' Stefano said, pointing to each in turn. 'Cakes in this one, bread in that one.'

Closer to her was a long glassed-in counter, filled with cake racks and bulging with goodies. Near to the door were two small circular tables laden with yet more items for customers to browse and enjoy.

'Wizard bread — one bite and you're enchanted!' proclaimed a sign at one of the tables. Beside it lay Harry Potter phoenix cakes and Harry Potter pasta shaped like tiny broomsticks.

'I thought these might appeal to our younger customers,' Stefano explained, correctly interpreting Heidi's questioning look. 'Marco worked on that display last week.'

With so much to see and so many

people, going through Soleari's took several moments. She and Stefano were assailed from every side by customers and staff members, the latter trim in crisp white bakers' uniforms and hats and wide-eyed in blatant curiosity as to who the boss's young companion was. Hearing their chatter and sensing their goodwill, Heidi felt accepted, the more so as Stefano introduced her as, 'My second cousin, Heidi. Ruggiero and Sarah's daughter,' acknowledging her and her mother.

'They're not exactly in awe of you, are they?' Heidi remarked as she and Stefano mounted a well-lit staircase leading to the upper floors. To her surprise, she'd just seen an older female member of staff rumple her companion's blond hair and jab him in the ribs.

'Emilia was merely asking when she should start preparing the ingredients for my wedding cake,' Stefano answered, brown eyes bright with mischief. 'We go through here, that red door.'

Wondering if her face was as vermilion as the paint, Heidi walked across the first floor landing and pushed the door open, entering an airy room with a small cooking range and sink in one corner and a long wooden table stacked with glasses, crockery and cutlery in the other. There was an espresso machine by the door and two scrubbed tables under the window.

'This is our self-service section for the employees,' Stefano explained, coming to stand beside Heidi as she wandered to the window to look out across the square. 'Fresh bread, salads and pasta from what's on offer downstairs. They have their lunches here before we close for the siesta. We're not reopening this evening, so they'll be having a late lunch today. They won't be up here for another hour.'

'I see,' Heidi said, selfishly glad that she and Stefano would have the place to themselves.

'Of course, it's free to them,' Stefano went on, a half-smile lurking about his mouth. 'I find their feedback on the new recipes very instructive. Now what bread and salad would you like? Shall I cook us some fresh pasta?' Quickly, he reeled off several different kinds of bread, pastas, salads and sweets until Heidi threw up her hands in mock horror, calling, 'Enough! Surprise me,' she said.

5

Ten days later, at about the same time of day, Heidi was again upstairs in the staff lunch room, sitting at the table under the window and waiting with Alberto, one of Soleari's master bakers, as Stefano prepared their lunch. The grizzled, gray-bearded, stocky Alberto was having tortellini stuffed with Bologna sausage. Heidi was having a 'surprise'. It had become almost a tradition and part of her banter with Stefano. She had come to Soleari's for lunch with him every day and found herself vastly intrigued by the whole business. Unlike her father, Ruggiero, she was eager to learn more. She now knew for instance that Soleari's was a *panetteria*, and that here in Bologna and in contrast to other cities in Italy, businesses like Soleari's, specializing in bread, also sold pasta, the fresh pasta made by hand.

'Stefano tells me you know about

scents and have a good nose. Smell that.'
Alberto finished pouring her a glass of
dark red wine and pushed it across the
table to her. 'Smell. Taste. Tell me what
you think.'

Heidi slowly swirled the wine in the
glass, thinking about Stefano. In the two
weeks she had known him she had discovered that under his rather shy reserve
was a kind, good man. There was a
sort of serious beauty about him, she
thought, pretending to study the wine
while watching Stefano. In profile, he
was like a medieval woodcut, all long,
clear lines. He'd broken off from tending
his simmering pans to remove his spectacles and peer at the inside of Emilia's
watch, which she said was losing time.
While Emilia stood close by, her thin-
plastic-gloved hands white with icing
sugar, Stefano did something to the
intricate mechanism with a small screw-
driver and then returned the watch to
her with a 'There you go,' as he replaced
his spectacles.

Yes, I really like Stefano, Heidi thought,

pleased to admit this to herself. She liked Rosa, too, and not only because she was now treating her older cousin. Rosa was still too shy for a full body massage with essential oils, but Heidi massaged her hands and feet, and today, after lunch, she would be working on her back for the first time. Rosa was not very talkative, but she had admitted to Heidi that she often felt 'poorly' and, in tones of deep apology, had confessed to a range of debilitating symptoms. After restocking her basic 'travel-kit' of oils in the city with Stefano's occasional help in translation, Heidi was treating Rosa with a mixture of essential oils for depression, lack of energy, palpitations and 'various problems with my monthly cycle', which Heidi had investigated further with several tactful questions. She thought that Rosa was beginning to look less strained and had already decided that she would try to persuade her to see her own doctor again and also to consider contacting a local aromatherapist.

'What do you think?' Alberto barked,

breaking into her reverie and returning Heidi to the business of savoring her wine.

'Good balance between fruitiness and woodiness,' Heidi replied, almost automatically, still shy of using the language of wine. In the farm in Yorkshire, they had drunk copious amounts of tea, but no wine. Even one of these tall glasses was sufficient to make her faintly light-headed. Or was that due to the fact that Stefano had just looked up from his deft serving out to give her an encouraging nod?

'Not a very robust fragrance but a faint fizz,' Heidi went on, raising her glass and sipping the wine. 'You can taste the grapes. I like it.'

'Naturally you like it, that's Lambrusco from our region!' said Alberto, trying to scowl but failing. 'The word is bouquet, not fragrance. Ah! Our pasta!'

Stefano placed Heidi's and Alberto's dishes in front of them and came to join them with his own steaming plate of tortellini. 'Be honest in what you think of your surprise,' he told Heidi, raising his glass of Lambrusco to her.

Heidi ate one of the mysterious little parcels from her dish, aware of Stefano's frequent glances at her and of Alberto's vigorous exclamations.

'The finest food in the world!' the master baker was saying. 'Only to be compared with our bread!' He thrust his now empty fork in Heidi's direction. 'She has a good nose, Stefano, and I think she will have the touch. A baker is nothing without the touch, the feel for the dough,' Alberto explained, catching Heidi's puzzled look. 'I think you should tell her, Stefano. You need help from someone in your family.'

Heidi said nothing. She knew from various dark hints from the other staff members and from Stefano that all was not right with Soleari's.

'If Heidi tells me what she thinks of my latest pasta first,' Stefano replied.

'Be serious,' Alberto growled.

'No, it's all right.' Heidi found herself defending Stefano. 'If this is to be a possible new range of pasta for Soleari's then feedback is important.' She tasted again. 'I like the faint aniseed flavor mingled with that creaminess. It's refreshing and mouth-filling.' She nodded. 'It's good.'

'Tortellini with roasted fennel, garlic and local goat's cheese filling,' Stefano confirmed. 'Glad you like it.'

'Not traditional,' muttered Alberto. He jabbed a thick finger at Stefano. 'Tell her what's happening. There's no one else up here now and I suppose Artemisia and Marco haven't graced us with their presence.'

'Not yet.' Stefano wiped his mouth with his napkin and looked at Heidi again as if sizing her up. 'Do you want to get dragged in?'

'One thing.' Alberto broke in before Heidi could respond. 'Why are you called Heidi? Is that a common English name?'

'No, Swiss. My mother loved the story of the little mountain girl and named me after her.' Heidi turned in her seat to face Stefano. 'I'd like to help, if I can.'

In a low, steady voice Stefano began to explain. 'Soleari's is a family business that has lasted over a hundred years. All members of the family down the paternal line have voting rights. Federico and Rosa are now retired. I look after the baking.'

'The creative side,' dropped in Alberto, finishing off his tortellini.

'Artemisia is in charge of the accounts and our younger brother, Marco, does the packaging and design. He arranges the main window and writes all the labels. Those have proved very popular.'

'Frippery!' Alberto snorted, and he scratched at his gray beard.

Heidi thought of the witty, rather suggestive descriptive tags that she'd read in the window and wondered what she would make of their author when she finally met the elusive Marco.

'Recently, my brother has been very actively courted by the management of a massive international bakery who would like to buy Soleari's out,' Stefano went on. 'They are talking a great deal of money, but it would mean a fundamental change in what Soleari's would produce.'

'Plastic bread merchants! Pah!' said Alberto, slapping a massive palm onto the table.

'They have assured Marco that they would still produce some very exclusive hand-made bread, and that has brought Artemisia round to the idea,' Stefano went on.

'Would this hand-made bread be very expensive?' Heidi asked, not in the least surprised when Stefano gave a grim nod. She thought of the other small bread shops and pasta shops that she had seen in Bologna, all proud to display their individually made, regional wares. 'Surely that kind of bland, international bread isn't what people want, is it?'

'No, you're right,' Stefano agreed. 'Marco's plan is against the history and tradition of Soleari's and even against modern trends in the baking trade.'

'People want real bread,' said Alberto. 'Why does Marco want to change?'

Heidi asked, eating more fennel and goat's cheese tortellini. She saw Stefano and Alberto exchange a look. 'Sorry, you don't have to tell me.'

'Marco has significant debts. Gambling debts that our parents, especially our mother, know little about,' said Stefano, in a hard, colorless voice. 'If the international bakery bought Soleari's out, then his share of that money would clear all his problems.'

'And he couldn't gradually pay off the debts?' Heidi asked, thinking about the number of times when money had been very tight on her grandparents' farm. 'You couldn't just leave the business as it is? It seems very successful.'

'It is.' Stefano drained off his glass of wine and poured another. Taking a deep breath, he said, 'The second oven has a fault in its stone base that's getting worse. It will soon need repairing, or better, replacing. But that will mean Soleari's closing for a time and a loss in revenues that neither Marco nor Artemisia will agree to. At the next family board meeting, they will propose that we sell the bakery.'

'Surely Federico and Rosa would never agree with that?'

'I don't know,' Stefano admitted. 'Marco can be very persuasive. Rosa has never felt part of the business — Federico has been very old-fashioned and excluded her from any real decisions — and now he himself doesn't seem particularly interested anymore.' Stefano's thin features seemed to lengthen and grow haggard as he frowned. 'Perhaps Marco and Artemisia know their parents' true minds more clearly than I do.'

Heidi thought this a strange statement, but she was shocked by what Stefano said next.

'You can have voting rights at the next family meeting, if you wish.'

'Me?'

'Through Ruggiero your father. So far as I know you will still have full voting rights.'

'So use them well, little Heidi.' Alberto rose stiffly to his feet and headed for the sink with his plate.

'I'll wash up,' Heidi quickly volunteered, part of her still astonished by what she had just learned. She was alarmed at what was at stake, and just a little chilled. Was this why Stefano seemed interested in her — because of her voting rights?

★　★　★

Soon afterwards, Stefano and Alberto had to go downstairs as Emilia called up a series of questions from a regular customer that only they could answer. Alone in the staff room, Heidi gave herself a talking to as she washed up, recalling the first time Stefano had met her. Then, he'd invited her out before he'd even known who she was.

'Heidi? Are you ready?' Stefano called out from the bottom of the stairs.

'Coming.' Heidi sped off down the steps with a will. She found it hard to think badly of Stefano, and now, when he met her at the base of the staircase and held out his hand to her, she took it at once, glad of the contact.

'Thanks for lunch,' she told him.

'My pleasure,' Stefano said, with a smile. 'Shall we go?'

Arm in arm they walked through Soleari's, Heidi feeling proud of her tall, blond companion. They reached the door at the same time as a small, red-cheeked elderly man, smartly turned out in tweeds, who walked with a stick.

'Good to see you about again, after your operation, Signor Bartoli.' Stefano stood back and opened the door, but the old man made a shooing motion at Heidi with his checked shopping bag.

'Your young lady first, Stefano. I'm surprised at you!' he exclaimed, raising and lowering his walking stick. 'After you, my dear.'

'Thank you.' Heidi went ahead, stopping outside as the glare of the afternoon sun through the arcade struck her eyes. She heard the elderly gentleman's shuffling steps as he limped out of the *panetteria* and turned to guide him off the pavement if he needed it. Over his head, she caught a glimpse of Stefano also leaving the shop and then realized that Signor Bartoli was going the other way, towards a square black shadow that had appeared before Soleari's main window.

Except that it wasn't a shadow, Heidi realized, moving as she understood what she was looking at. 'Signore! Wait! Stefano!' She appealed instinctively to him as her reaching hand closed around the old man's upper arm, pulling Signor Bartoli back from the newly-revealed gaping drop in the pavement.

'I've got you,' she heard Stefano say and sensed rather than saw Stefano's strong, wiry arms enclose around the old man, lifting Signor Bartoli right off his feet as Stefano fought to draw him to safety.

For an instant all three of them hovered on the brink of the drop. Heidi saw the black hole in front of her seem to widen and deepen. She felt as if it was actually sucking her down, her and Signor Bartoli.

'No!' The protest burst from her. She stiffened, bracing her legs, and deliberately stepped backwards, keeping a tight hold of the man's arm. She felt a rush of air, a shift in her weight and then she and Signor Bartoli were standing safely on the pavement, with Stefano gripping them both.

'All you okay?' she asked, as he asked her the same question.

Stefano nodded, saying, 'Are you?'

'Fine. A little shaken, but fine.' Heidi retrieved Signor Bartoli's walking stick, which had not fallen into the cellar but rolled into the gutter.

'Signore?' Stefano asked.

'Yes, yes! You can let go of me, Stefano. I'm not going to jump into the cellar today.' Signor Bartoli's red cheeks had paled slightly, but otherwise he was unhurt. 'Thank you, my dear,' he said, as Heidi handed him his walking stick, patting her hand.

'I think I will go the other way around the square,' he announced, and with an almost courtly bow to Heidi, he walked off in the opposite direction.

'That was lucky,' Heidi remarked, absently rubbing her smarting arm.

Stefano was closing the trapdoor. He didn't say anything until the wooden door was firmly in place. Then he looked at her. 'Are you sure you're all right?'

'Yes,' Heidi said gently, thinking that he looked strained. When he moved, he flinched, catching his breath and automatically rubbing his side.

'It's nothing,' he said, as Heidi came closer to help. 'I felt a twinge in my side when I caught Signor Bartoli. It'll go off in a minute. Can you wait here? I need to find out which idiot opened the cellar door and left it unattended.'

He was gone before Heidi could respond, disappearing back into Soleari's. She half-expected to hear furious shouting but instead Stefano seemed to be having a quiet word with each member of staff. He joined her a moment later, busily polishing his spectacles with his clean handkerchief.

'None of my people say they opened

the cellar trapdoor, and I believe them,' he said starkly.

'But then who would do such a thing?' Heidi asked. 'Signor Bartoli could have had a very nasty fall —'

'— and Soleari's would have been responsible,' Stefano finished for her.

Visions of law suits and crippling damages flashed in Heidi's mind. Shocked, for an instant she could not speak.

'That's the second time this month,' Stefano went on.

'What do you mean?'

Scowling, Stefano replaced his spectacles. 'Can I explain on the way home? This isn't something I want to talk about in the open square.'

'Of course.' Heidi stifled her questions as she and Stefano began to walk across the square, Stefano wincing for the first few steps until he realized that she was watching him.

'I'd like to take a taxi home,' Heidi said then. 'I'm still a bit shaken up. Look. There's a taxi rank just over there.' To her relief, Stefano did not protest and let her lead the way across the sun-bleached flagstones.

6

Later, in the villa garden, after she had given Rosa her latest aromatherapy session, Heidi strolled with Stefano about the terraces and talked. Usually their talks were easy, with neither at a loss for conversation, but today, after the almost fatal 'accident' outside Soleari's, matters were very different. Walking with hunched shoulders and with none of his usual slim grace, Stefano spoke in a low rasping monotone.

He told her of several odd incidents and 'accidents' at Soleari's over the past two months that seemed too small and occasional to be sabotage but were nonetheless disturbing. Like Signor Bartoli, who could have fallen headlong into their cellar through the open trapdoor. Two weeks ago Signora Cardenli's beloved toy poodle, Nix, had been violently ill after eating one of Soleari's vol-au-vents, something the little dog had eaten many times before with no problem. The vet had told an anxious Signora Cardenli that the savory must have been tainted in some way, which an appalled Stefano could not believe. Their hygiene and methods were very strict. Luckily, the signora had accepted his explanation, and there had been no more incidents of that sort, but he was uneasy.

'What do you think it could have been?' Heidi asked at this point.

Stefano shrugged, a rare expressive gesture for him and one which starkly revealed his inner agitation. 'Perhaps the poodle was already sick. Or perhaps someone had spiked the pastry.'

'Who would do that? How?' Even as she spoke, Heidi was remembering how busy the shop was, how many customers there could be milling about both inside and out. Purchases were always elaborately bagged but perhaps someone had bought exactly what the signora had bought, slipped into a side-street, applied a few drops of weed-killer or another irritant and then resealed the bag and somehow swapped it with Signora Cardenli's.

Heidi scowled at the idea. It was too complicated, surely. But otherwise that would mean either that the pastry had been off — something she believed no more than did Stefano — or a member of staff had done it. 'That's terrible,' she murmured.

'There's more,' Stefano said heavily. Timers had been found mysteriously switched on or off and no one knew who had done it. On another occasion, a whole batch of olive focacce had to be thrown away, their crusts burnt and blackened beyond recognition.

'I've talked to Alberto, Emilia, and young Gina,' Stefano went on, naming the three regular members of staff. 'None of them remember seeing anything suspicious during these incidents and I can't believe they would have anything to do with them. Alberto and Emilia have been part of the business for years, and Gina is engaged and talks of nothing but her forthcoming marriage.' A tolerant light hovered in Stefano's warm brown eyes. 'I'd say baking is the last thing on her mind, but she's not careless.'

Heidi agreed. She was sure that none of Soleari's employees would be careless.

'What about — ?' she began, and stopped, blushing at the thought of her own tactlessness.

'What about Marco and Artemisia?' Stefano finished for her.

By this time they had reached a terrace with a small fountain that blew a cooling spray over Heidi's scalding cheeks. Careless of the teasing spray, she stopped in front of the fountain, in the shade of a gnarled pine tree, twisted out of shape by the prevailing wind, and raised anxious eyes to her companion. 'I'm sorry. That was insulting and unfair, especially when I'm not even a member of this family.'

A curious look of shame and alarm shadowed briefly across Stefano's face, but it was gone as he took her hand in both of his. 'You are family, Heidi. We all think so. You are family far more — well, than some of us,' he finished obliquely. 'As for Artemisia and Marco, why should they sabotage the bakery? They may differ in their plans for the business, but don't forget they would lose out, too if Soleari's reputation suffered. The big international bakery might even withdraw its offer if these incidents became common knowledge.'

He was standing right in front of her, so close that she could see the definition of his lean, muscular frame through his crisp cotton shirt. 'Yes, I can see that,' Heidi said, exasperated at herself. She would never agree to massage a fully naked man but she dealt with male clients in her aromatherapy practice, treated their hands and feet, their necks and shoulders. Why should she be so flustered by Stefano? 'How's your sprain?' she asked, seizing gratefully on the change of subject.

'Better for this gentle walk,' Stefano said, in a voice of amused indulgence. 'But if you are offering to treat my aching shoulder and back . . .'

His smile deepened as Heidi was silent, torn between her professional life and this strange new shyness she seemed to have acquired while dealing with him.. Perhaps it was because he had opened up to her a little and now, standing by this fountain, he was as close as her own shadow. Closer, because he was lowering that bright blond head and his clever, sensitive hands were encircling her narrow waist . . .

He kissed her lightly on the mouth and brushed a bead of fountain spray from her cheek. 'I've wanted to do that for a long time,' he said, kissing her again. He smelled of fresh bread and sun and his hands on her back held her tenderly, as if she was made of spun sugar.

'Don't you know how very pretty you are?' he said softly, laughing as she stiffened at the compliment. 'You are, you know. Like the little bride doll on top of a wedding cake.' Stefano blushed, clearly embarrassed at hearing himself say anything, so absurdly sentimental. 'Thank you for your help,' he said gruffly, taking a step back and releasing her.

It was only a thank you kiss, Heidi told herself. She'd known Stefano for only two weeks. *What does that matter?* an inner voice whispered, but Heidi ignored the voice and tried to control her rapidly beating heart, taking several slow deep breaths. 'Shall we continue our walk?' she said, grateful that her question was not a squeak.

Stefano stood back and pointed down the gravelled path. 'There you go.'

Moving first, Heidi set off along the path, scarcely conscious of the wafting spray from the fountain or the opulent red peonies and roses lining the terrace walkway. Stefano had kissed her. She touched her lips with her hand, feeling truly sensual for the first time in her life, registering that she was wearing a blue cotton button-through sundress and sandals, items that had just become her favorite outfit.

'Hey, wait!' Stefano overtook her in a few strides. 'It's usually you trotting after me,' he teased.

'Pardon me, but I don't trot.' Feeling more composed, Heidi took Stefano's hand in hers. 'Got you!' she teased in return. 'Where to now?'

★ ★ ★

Stefano's smile deepened. They could get lost in the garden for hours so far as he was concerned. 'You decide,' he answered, part of him astonished at how easily his serious concerns over Soleari's and his persistent, nagging doubts at his own place within the family seemed to have gone on holiday for the afternoon, ever since he'd kissed Heidi.

'This way.' Heidi pointed to a small grassy path that led farther down the garden, through a rockery and past several statues. As she moved, her long hair shimmered on her shoulders like black silk. I wonder what it feels like? Stefano thought, longing to touch it.

'Have you any ideas who might be behind these incidents at Soleari's?' she asked, her question brutally reminding

Stefano of his responsibilities.

He sighed and admitted the truth, 'I don't know. I was hoping —'

But the rest of his thought was interrupted by a new, cheery voice calling in charmingly Italian-accented English, 'Hello, my beautiful Heidi! How are you? Step away from gloomy Stefano there and come up into the sunshine with me!'

Inwardly cursing, conscious of an emotion that he would not admit was jealousy, Stefano fixed a smile upon his face and prepared to introduce Heidi to his younger, handsome brother, Marco.

* * *

Standing on a higher terrace above them with the sun outlining his sleek designer jeans and open-necked shirt was the most handsome man Heidi had ever seen, a dark Brad Pitt with a winning smile and expansive gestures. When she and Stefano reached this smiling individual and Stefano gave stiff introductions, 'Heidi, this is my brother Marco. Marco,

Heidi —' Marco immediately swept her off her feet, whirling her about.

'Our sweet and dainty Heidi!' he exclaimed, so loudly that a roosting pigeon in one of the nearby laurels took flight in a noisy flutter of wings. 'Arte said you were tiny, but I'd no idea you'd be so enchanting.'

'Now that is too much!' Heidi said laughing, when her exuberant cousin finally set her back down on her feet. But Marco was not to be quelled. Dark eyes sparkling with mischief, he said, 'That's only my beginning, Heidi. Heidi. Have you an Italian name?'

'My middle name is Maria,' Heidi replied, glancing at Stefano for guidance but receiving no sign from him. He was wearing his frozen aristocratic mask again. The two brothers could hardly be less like each other, she thought.

'Maria.' Marco tapped his pursed lips with a finger. 'You are certainly dark enough to be a Maria, and my mother tells me you have our grandfather's looks.' He clapped his hands together. 'I shall call you Heidi Maria.'

'Marco, she isn't used to your ways,' Stefano said, but Marco brushed his protest aside with a muttered, 'Don't be your usual kill-joy,' in Italian.

'Should I call you Marco Federico then?' Heidi asked blandly, in perfect Italian. She was rewarded with a swift, hard-to-read look from Stefano and a shout of laughter from his brother.

'You are one of the family! Very much of the blood. And now you must let me take you to dinner at Roberto's. I insist,' he added, with a smile, as Heidi drew in a breath. 'In celebration of your prodigal return. What do you say?'

Again, Heidi looked at Stefano, who merely said, 'I haven't the time. I've lots of paperwork to get through tonight.' He shot a steely glance at his brother. 'You should be helping me with this. Packaging is your area. Where've you been these last few days anyway?'

'Computer conference looking at the latest digital design techniques. I did leave a note on your desk,' Marco said, utterly unabashed by Stefano's glare.

'Strange that I couldn't find it then,' Stefano said, and Marco agreed, 'Isn't it?' then turned to Heidi. 'What do you say? Don't let Stefano put you off.'

'Of course Heidi can go if she wants to,' Stefano said, in a dry, formal way that made Heidi want to yell at him, 'We kissed earlier this afternoon, or have you forgotten?' Perhaps it meant nothing to him. Or more likely, Marco was being deliberately provocative in that way of sibling rivalry that she'd seen so often amongst her friends in Britain and Stefano was reacting badly to that.

'I'm not sure,' she began, not wanting to seem a misery in the face of such obvious good humor. 'Your mother may have plans that involve me.'

'Oh, you needn't worry about Mamma. She knows I've booked us a table. Please say you'll come!' Marco exclaimed, dropping onto his knees on the path in front of her. 'Roberto would never forgive me if I didn't turn up at his restaurant tonight. He takes all cancellations as a personal insult.'

Embarrassed by this show, Heidi covered her shyness with a joke. 'If you stay on your knees much longer you'll take root. I'll be pleased to come with you. Is Artemisia coming, too?'

'No, no, just us,' Marco said, springing to his feet.

'Excuse me.' Stefano stepped back from both of them. 'I have work.'

He turned and was gone, vanishing between the bushy shrubs and brilliant flowers into the deeper tree shade.

'He's going the wrong way for the house,' Marco observed needlessly.

Anxiously wondering why Stefano was acting as he was, Heidi said nothing.

* * *

The food at Roberto's brightly lit and expensive restaurant on Bologna's main square might have been delicious, but Heidi scarcely tasted it. Conscious of her simple black dress, she felt uneasy and out of place beside the gleaming gowns and smart bespoke casuals of Bologna's fashionable people. She missed Stefano, with a sharpness that surprised and worried her. As a dinner companion, Marco was spasmodically attentive and seemed reasonably eager to please, but she remained wary of him, perhaps because to someone as good looking as he was and as used to being stared at wherever he went, everything was a show. Heidi knew she was a novelty, another girl for him to be seen with as he chattered ostentatiously with Roberto himself and greeted and air-kissed several beautiful women coming into the restaurant with their older, Armani-suited escorts. Each time he did this, Marco seemed to recall who he was with and would slip deftly back into his seat to ask if she needed help in understanding the menu, or choosing the wine, or inquiring if she was comfortable. To all of which Heidi gave polite, neutral replies.

When their food arrived, Marco finally settled in his seat and began to tell her stories about the family. He told her about Rosa's first attempt to make a Sicilian-style pizza, which she over-cooked and finished feeding to the birds. He told her about Artemisia's confirmation, where as his sister was walking about in the garden, proudly showing off her beautiful flounced white dress, one of the scarlet bows became entangled in a rose bush. 'Stefano cut her free with a pair of kitchen scissors, with Arte alternately shouting at him and crying because her dress was having to be cut,' Marco finished.

'My own confirmation the next year wasn't much better,' he went on. 'I managed to fall on my behind in my new trousers and went into church looking an absolute urchin.'

Heidi laughed at his story. When he grinned like that, Marco was very appealing and would have made a charming urchin. She guessed he was about her own age and briefly envied him his supportive and clearly indulgent family. 'What about your older brother's confirmation?' she could not resist asking, thinking how painstaking Stefano would have been in helping to free Artemisia from the rose.

Marco shrugged. 'I don't know anything about that,' he said dismissively. 'That would have been at the orphanage. Didn't you know?' His young, handsome face gleamed in the dazzle of Roberto's wall and ceiling lights, 'Has none of the family told you yet? Stefano's adopted. His parents were killed in a car wreck when he was seven, and he was at various foster homes and orphanages until he was nine. My parents decided to take him because they'd been told that Rosa was unlikely to conceive and they thought they couldn't have children of their own. They visited the orphanage soon afterwards and saw Stefano. Rosa thought he looked lonely and felt sorry for him and persuaded Federico to take him instead of a toddler or a cute baby. Life being what it is, one year later, Mamma had Arte, and then, a year after that, she became pregnant with me.'

Marco leaned across the table towards

her, clearly relishing her silence and shock. 'Didn't you wonder why he was so different from us in coloring and looks?'

'Artemisia . . .' Heidi stammered, still trying to absorb what Marco had told her. Shocked by the casual, almost callous way he had described these tragic events, she was stunned that he'd said anything. It seemed almost deliberately cruel. 'Artemisia has auburn hair.'

'Skillful dyeing,' Marco told her, pressing the tips of his fingers together and looking at her over their table lamp. 'Arte's as dark as I am, or you.'

Marco waved a finger at her plate. 'Have you finished your antipasta?' he asked gently, referring to her half-eaten first course of shellfish salad.

'Yes, thank you.' Heidi put her fork and spoon together and pressed her damask napkin to her trembling mouth, hoping that Marco would not see how upset she was. There were two more courses to get through, and she did not know how she would manage. Following Marco's revelation, her appetite had deserted her.

'Yes, I'm sure that's why my good brother is so very serious,' Marco continued, raising a hand to alert one of the slim, sleek waiters. 'I remember when we were younger, how he was always trying to prove himself.'

Heidi said nothing. She now knew whom Marco reminded her of, Steve Todd, one of the young farmers who had inherited a property close to her childhood home near Selby. Steve Todd was handsome and much sought after by all the young women of the area but Heidi had never liked him, especially after she had seen him striding about his fields with a gun, shooting rabbits and crows and kestrels. 'He's only being a good manager of his land and getting rid of vermin,' her grandfather had said, when Heidi had furiously protested, but she'd never forgotten the gloating, avid look on Steve Todd's face as he wandered around his property, carrying his gun.

Marco's movie-star face had the same expression as he added, just as a young bearded waiter began to approach their table, 'Of course, my parents are delighted with Stefano, and they'd be even more delighted if he and Arte would hurry up and announce their engagement. I'd say it's an understood thing, really. Now, what will you have as your main course?'

7

Heidi struggled through the rest of the evening, and later she thanked Marco for a dinner which she would have done much to miss. Marco's words about Stefano and Artemisia were impossible to forget. No matter how many times she told herself that the evidence of her own senses proved that Marco's supposition was unlikely, her mind kept dwelling on their soon-to-be announced engagement. If nothing else, it would keep Soleari's securely within the family, and Stefano was certainly committed to the business.

That night Heidi slept badly. Her next shock was delivered the following morning by Stefano himself, during their pre-breakfast drink together in the kitchen.

'Sorry, but we can't have lunch together today,' he said, frowning at her through his spectacles. He dragged a hand through his wavy thatch of hair. There were rings of tiredness under his eyes. Heidi longed to comfort him.

'That's okay,' she said reasonably. 'There's always tomorrow. How's the sprain?' she added, irritated as she felt a blush rising up her face.

'Gone,' Stefano said tersely, but he didn't look pleased. If anything, he looked even more unhappy. 'No, I'm sorry, lunch together just isn't possible, not for all the rest of this week. So much is happening that I can't. I have to be places, somewhere else.'

Heidi waited, but he did not elaborate, just hid his drawn face behind his coffee mug. When she asked gently, 'Is it anything to do with what we've talked about earlier?' he leapt to his feet and left the kitchen table. 'I have to go now, back to Soleari's.

'Will you see to this morning's rolls for me?' He waved a distracted arm in the direction of the oven.

'I'll be glad to help,' Heidi told him, and she was. She was grateful that

Stefano trusted her to look after the freshly-baked bread that she and the rest of the family would soon be enjoying for breakfast. All the family except for Stefano, who'd made them, patiently explaining each step of the process.

So if he could do that, why could he not tell me that he was adopted?

'Good luck,' she told him as he left.

He turned on the threshold and gave her the first genuine smile she had seen that morning. 'Thank you,' he said. Striding back into the kitchen, he leaned down and kissed her forehead. He seemed on the verge of saying something, but then he shook his head and walked away, back into the villa, possibly to retrieve the briefcase she'd seen him put ready to pick up as he left by the front door.

Alone, Heidi had only a few moments to dwell on her disappointment before a gentle cough alerted her to the presence of another family member. Raising her head from her lukewarm cup of tea, she saw Rosa standing on the kitchen threshold where Stefano had stood and forced herself to smile.

'Hello! How are you?' she asked, noting that Rosa seemed less pale than she had been and that there was a new brightness about her bobbed cap of sleek brown hair. Today, Rosa was dressed more colorfully than on previous occasions, in a tailored wool dress in a rich tangerine.

'I like the dress,' Heidi went on. 'Is it new?'

'Yes, it is.' Rosa plucked a soft tangerine pleat, adding in quiet Italian, 'Federico would once have noticed it was new,' before reverting to English, in a brisker manner, 'I am becoming well, thank you. Your treatments are helping me.'

'That's good,' Heidi said, pleased to have her instincts confirmed. Sensing that Rosa wanted to talk, she was keen to keep this spasmodic conversation going. 'Are you and Federico driving anywhere today?'

While she had been staying at the

villa, Federico and Rosa had gone off on morning sight-seeing trips to various little towns and villages close to Bologna in the Emilia Romania region. Federico called it, 'Learning my own country,' and even if Artemisia scoffed and accused her parents of being the 'most unimaginative pair of retirees I know,' Heidi thought that what they were doing was charming.

'I-I think so.' Rosa started as the old timer that Stefano used to remind him to check the bread — not that he ever needed reminding, so far as Heidi knew — suddenly went off with a noisy buzz.

'Excuse me.' Hoping that Rosa would soon enter her own kitchen, Heidi switched off the timer and walked across the tiles to the oven. 'Stefano had to leave early this morning,' she explained over her shoulder as she opened the oven door and the fragrance of fresh bread blossomed in the room. 'He left me in charge of the rolls this morning.'

She lifted the bread out and tapped and

tested each roll, piling them deftly onto a rack to cool. Behind her, she sensed a change of air as Rosa approached, heard her say in her low, diffident way, 'You move like Stefano around bread.'

'Oh, he showed me every step.'

'No, no. I mean you have the touch. You're not afraid of it.'

Heidi turned to stare at Rosa. She had sat down at the kitchen table where Stefano had been sitting. She was turning a teaspoon over and over on the well-scrubbed wood.

'I thought Federico would be right about you,' Rosa continued, still turning the spoon. 'I know what your hands can do.'

Embarrassed, Heidi plunged the empty baking trays into the cold water in the sink, where they sizzled and steamed. Strangely, as she grew shyer, Rosa seemed to become more confident, her voice becoming clearer.

'We have talked about it again, Federico and I, and we decided last night that it was the right thing; the just thing to do.

We are resurrecting Ruggiero's old voting rights within the business and giving them to you.'

Suddenly Heidi discovered that she wanted to sit down. Stefano had mentioned voting rights to her as something she *could* have, but Rosa's statement made it clear that these rights were now something she *did* have. 'Are you sure?' She settled less than gracefully onto a stool. Her heart drummed inside her as she wondered how many other surprises this family would launch at her. 'What about the others? What does Stefano think?'

'Stefano knows, of course,' Rosa said. In contrast to Heidi's breathless state, Rosa seemed calm, pleased to have got the matter out of the way. 'Federico talked to him and Artemisia last night. Marco, too, after you had both come in from the restaurant.' Rosa laid the teaspoon down in front of her place and looked straight at Heidi with a gentle smile. 'Stefano approves.'

'I see,' Heidi said faintly. 'But I really

know nothing about the business. I didn't even know that Soleari's is a *panetteria*, not a bread shop.'

Rosa's smile widened. 'But you are learning, yes?'

'I think so. I'm trying. Stefano really approves?'

'As do the others,' Rosa added swiftly, in a way that told Heidi that Marco and Artemisia — Artemisia probably — were less happy with this development. Still, she could not help rejoicing that Stefano was pleased. She valued his approval above all.

'You like Stefano, I think,' Rosa said, scrutinizing Heidi in a way that Heidi wasn't sure she felt entirely comfortable with. 'He is, as I am sure he has told you by now, adopted.'

'I know,' said Heidi. *Only not from Stefano*.

'But he is always very much a son to me,' Rosa went on. 'And of course, even if you were related, you would be second cousins, not so close by blood. Stefano's a good boy. Always very serious, although he can laugh.'

'Stefano? I can certainly make him laugh.' Artemisia entered the kitchen in another flowing kimono, this one in shocking pink silk. She claimed her mother for a kiss.

'Yes, *cara*, I know you can,' Rosa said fondly, staring up at her beautiful daughter with obvious pride and admiration. 'But then you and Stefano have such a special relationship.'

Artemisia smiled and kissed her mother again, declaring, 'Are those the breakfast rolls? I'm starving! Mamma, will you join me in having a coffee, some espresso before Papa and Marco come down and try to make us wait on them?'

'Excuse me,' Heidi said quietly, determined to slip away to her bedroom before anything else was said.

Mounting the marble staircase to the upper rooms, she felt she needed a moment to re-gather her composure as she wondered just how close Stefano and Artemisia really were. Had Rosa's mention of Stefano's adoption been meant as approval of her involvement with him? Or had Rosa's comment on Stefano's and Artemisia's 'special relationship' perhaps been Rosa's way of warning her off? If so, Heidi knew that any warning was already too late.

I'm falling in love with him, she thought, and a great sense of wonder rushed through her in a dizzying surge of joy. 'Stefano Soleari, the adopted son,' she said aloud softly as she entered her room, then walked to the window and looked down over the city, down into Bologna where Stefano was.

★ ★ ★

Feeling as she did, Heidi was torn between hope and dread that Stefano might notice how she now regarded him. Conscious of her spirits lifting each time she thought he might step into the same room or street as herself, she treasured the most fleeting glimpses of his tall, rangy figure.

Which was just as well, Heidi admitted

wryly because she saw little of Stefano over the following days. No matter how early she slipped down to the kitchen, he was gone. Sometimes she doubted if he even returned from Soleari's after the night-baking. He did not return to the villa until late at night. Over the first couple of days, Heidi had walked down to Soleari's, but found that Stefano was not there. She had either just missed him or he'd not been there since the early morning. She did not feel she could impose herself on him during the night-time baking session, but she missed him very much, the more so because she wasn't certain that he ever thought of her.

As a further disappointment, Federico had taken over the ritual of the morning rolls. He was as good a bread-maker as his son, Heidi reluctantly admitted, and he always greeted her with a big smile, but unlike Stefano, he would not allow her to help. Perhaps he did not think she had 'the touch', Heidi thought sourly, and then berated herself for being so petty. This was the family she'd craved and longed to know about over the years, and they had welcomed her into their home. She should be grateful and happy. Besides, Federico had trusted her enough to agree to give her the old voting rights that had once belonged to her father and wasn't that something?

Even so, as the days drew on and Heidi walked about the city, chatted with the family and treated Rosa in her regular aromatherapy sessions, she began to wonder why she was staying. This was her first holiday for five years, and although Bologna was a marvelous city, filled with the wonderful arcades, markets and shops that she loved, Heidi found her eyes straying to the hills beyond. There was a whole region to explore, Venice and Parma and Florence, cities that she'd always wanted to see, and only a train ride away.

Rosa, meanwhile, had tentatively invited her to go with her and Federico on their morning drives, but Heidi had smilingly declined. She knew that whatever Stefano had said, Rosa was uneasy in her marriage, and she felt that Rosa and Federico might resolve whatever it was if they were left alone.

There was another, more sulky reason that Heidi only shared with herself as she scowled at her reflection in her bedroom mirror. If she was going to see Italy with any of this family, she wanted it to be with Stefano.

She appreciated that he was involved with the business, and she understood why. If he had been able to throw aside the lives of people like Alberto and Emilia and customers like old Signor Bartoli, she would have thought less of him. But day after day dawned, and she and Stefano scarcely spoke to each other. It was as if their lunches and that sensual, tender kiss in the garden had never been.

Had Rosa or Artemisia 'had a word' with Stefano, perhaps? Had they reminded him that he was supposed to marry Artemisia?

Heidi didn't like that idea, and honestly didn't think it likely, but Marco's mocking words haunted her. Marco and

Artemisia themselves were equally distracting, in different ways. One morning, very early, Artemisia had appeared in the kitchen, dressed in a smart white cook's uniform and with her hair in a stunning French pleat and had proceeded to take over the baking of that morning's bread from her father, instructing Federico to go out into the garden to gather some roses for the table.

While her words reminded Heidi of when she had first met Stefano, Artemisia did not waste the chance of her father's absence to turn on her.

'I know what your plan is, Heidi, but it won't work,' she said bluntly, slapping her risen dough vigorously onto the flour-strewn table. 'Stefano isn't interested, Marco certainly isn't, and my parents will soon see through this caring-healing routine of yours. And I wouldn't feel too important about those voting rights, either. My father has a casting vote, so yours won't count.'

'So why are you so upset about it?' Heidi asked quietly.

'Who says I'm upset?' Artemisia snapped, kneading the dough with the palms of her hands. 'As far as I'm concerned, you're an irrelevance. You'll be gone in another three weeks, less if I have my way.'

'And that's what really eats at you, isn't it? Your lack of control,' Heidi said, knowing that her words would incense Artemisia further but unable to resist. Determined to say nothing more — she had no wish to be drawn into an all-out argument in a house where she was a guest — Heidi swiftly left Artemisia to vent the rest of her spite in private and walked out into the garden to find Federico. Later, it should have amused her that Artemisia's bread, although acceptable, was not as outstanding as Stefano's or Federico's, but instead she felt no sense of satisfaction, only a regret that she and Artemisia could not be friends. She was aggrieved that the beautiful, cultured and rather spoiled Artemisia clearly saw her as nothing more than an upstart on the make.

'If she thinks bread is hard, she ought to try milking cows,' Heidi muttered, and was still grinning at the thought as she ran down the garden terraces.

Marco was as stand-offish as his sister, although less overtly hostile. Since inviting her for dinner, Marco had largely ignored her, which Heidi found a relief in some ways but hurtful in others. He made her feel dull. Clearly she had been found wanting at Roberto's, and her handsome cousin had decided that she was worth no more of his time.

What Marco and Artemisia did with their time remained a mystery to Heidi, since it was clear that they spent virtually no time at Soleari's. At breakfast, Federico always asked if they were going into the 'bread-shop' — his new title for the panetteria and an indulgent teasing of Heidi — but when Marco and Artemisia said no or simply avoided answering, their father did not pursue it. Heidi could understand why Stefano felt that Federico had lost interest in the business and that saddened her, too, for

Stefano's sake.

Another day slipped by, which Heidi considered note-worthy only because Rosa talked to her during her aroma-therapy, hesitantly admitting that she was worried about Federico's regular absences on every Thursday afternoon.

'He won't tell me where he goes or what he does, and he always takes the car so I can't follow,' Rosa said unhappily, her pale face pressed against her pillow as Heidi massaged her back and shoulders with a blend of fragrant and healing oils. 'Ah! That lavender scent takes me back to when I was a girl on holiday in Venice on the Lido! Have I ever told you about that?'

'I don't think you have,' Heidi said, going along with the change of subject. She longed to tell Rosa not to worry, but here, along with the mysterious 'sabotage' at Soleari's and the puzzle of when Marco and Artemisia did any work there, was another enigma. Where did Federico go on Thursday afternoons?

★ ★ ★

That evening, long before dinner, Stefano came home much earlier than he had been doing. He sought her out in the music room, where she was slowly playing through, 'Come back to Sorrento,' a tune she remembered her father singing to her.

'There have been no more unexplained 'incidents' at Soleari's,' Stefano told her. 'I thought you'd be glad to know that.'

'Of course!' Heidi said, delighted that Stefano was here with her. 'That's great news!'

'What's that, Heidi-Maria, that you are coming to Venice tomorrow with me?' drawled Marco from the doorway. Ignoring his instantly grim-faced brother, he waltzed across to the piano to join them.

'Mamma told me how fascinated you were in her childhood travelers' tales and I thought that seeing I've been neglecting you,' — this said with a self-deprecating smile — 'that I would make amends

111

by whisking you off to see Saint Mark's Square and all of La Serenissima's other glories.'

'La Serenissima?' Heidi was bewildered by Marco's sudden invitation.

'He means Venice,' Stefano said shortly, stepping back from Heidi and turning on his heel. 'I'll leave you two to make your arrangements.'

'Wait.' Heidi started up from the piano stool but found her path blocked by Marco, who took her hand in his and swung it to and fro.

'I think an early start will be best,' Marco said. 'I've so much to show you.'

But Heidi had decided that she'd had enough. 'I'm sorry, Marco,' she said as softly as she could. 'I'm afraid I can't go with you tomorrow. I'm meeting Gina in town,' she lied. She felt as if he had deliberately manufactured their day in Venice to drive a wedge between herself and Stefano, and while she was disappointed at his small-minded malice, she was also irritated at Stefano for not realizing what his brother was doing.

How can an intelligent man be so blind? she thought indignantly, striding away from the music room to her own bedroom. She could feel an anger headache building and abruptly decided that she would plead off joining the family for dinner tonight. She would have a bath and an early night and try to decide what to do with the rest of her time in Italy. Now that Rosa was improving and the business seemed free of sabotage, how much longer should she stay? She remembered her grandmother's adage about good guests not outstaying their welcome and admitted wretchedly that perhaps it was time that she tore herself away from the Villa Rosa. *And from Stefano*, her thoughts whispered, but she could see no other way. If he could not even admit to her the basic truth of himself, of where he came from and who he was, what chance had they of any lasting relationship?

★ ★ ★

The delicious scents of minestrone soup and roast lamb wafting up from the kitchen turned Heidi faintly sick rather than hungry as later she sat on her bed in front of the wardrobe mirror to brush her hair. She had warded off the worst of the headache with a judicious use of essential oils on herself after her bath, but she was glad she had given Rosa her apologies for tonight.

A soft knock at her door. 'Heidi? Are you okay?'

'Come in if you like, Stefano,' she called out, her heart quickening as she heard his voice. She knew that her grandmother wouldn't have approved of her inviting him into her room, dressed as she was in her dressing gown, but she was after all twenty-one, and this was the twenty-first century. The dressing gown in question was one that enveloped her from head to foot in pale blue toweling so she was hardly immodest. Heidi felt strangely happy and rather reckless. 'Come in,' she said again, even as the door was opening.

'Mamma said you were unwell. What's wrong? Can I fetch you anything?'

Stefano's anxious face and questions soothed her more than her own healing oils. She drank in his concern like a thirsty flower accepting water but loved him too much to cause him grief. 'I'm feeling a little better, thanks,' she said, dropping her hairbrush on the bed and holding out a hand to him. 'Possibly a touch of sun. An early night will see me well again.'

'Is there anything you need? Here, let me brush your hair.'

Her hair was long, and felt longer still as Stefano's hands gently teased it free 'Is this okay?' he asked.

Heidi nodded, closing her eyes. The top of her head was tingling with a delicious tension, and the slow, gentle brushing of her hair made her feel stretched out and languorous. She wanted to ask him about himself, about his past, a way to show him that she was interested and possibly a way he would begin to talk about his adoption. Instead, before she even realized she was going to, she yawned.

'There you go.' Stefano dropped a kiss onto her forehead. 'Would you like anything else? No? Then I think I'd better leave. Sleep well, my Heidi.'

After he was gone, Heidi stretched out on the bed, closing her eyes and thinking of Stefano's smiling face. *My Heidi*. He had called her that.

'How can I think of leaving the Villa Rosa now?' she said aloud.

8

The next day Heidi woke full of renewed doubts. Stefano's continuing absence at breakfast did nothing to reassure her, and the fact that he had left no message for her made her wonder if last night had simply been a moment of physical attraction that meant nothing to him.

Marco was not in the kitchen when she came downstairs in her newly favorite blue button-through cotton dress, but any guilty pleasure she might have felt at her handsome relative's not pursuing her further with suggestions of a day trip to Venice was short lived.

'Heidi!' Artemisia called from upstairs, her voice echoing down over the marble balustrade of the staircase. 'Will you come up here a moment? I want you to see something.'

Her face calm for Federico, who was listening with wide-eyed interest, Heidi retraced her steps upstairs to the villa's bedrooms. Artemisia was waiting for her on the landing, and Heidi braced herself for whatever revelation was coming.

'Here, I wondered if you might like to borrow this while you're still staying with us.' Artemisia held out a Mexican sombrero-style sun-hat. 'Stefano bought it for me. He bought this for me, too, but I'm afraid I can't lend it to you.' She tapped a wide silver bangle on her wrist.

'Stefano's generous,' Heidi remarked coolly, well-aware of what Artemisia was doing. 'Thanks for the offer of the hat, but I'll be fine. Gina and I will be under-cover in town with all those arcades.' She checked her watch. 'I need to hurry if I'm not going to be late.'

Conscious of Artemisia watching, she walked along the landing to her own room, her thoughts remaining with that silver bangle. How did Stefano see himself within the family? As a brother by adoption or as an outsider? Was his gift to Artemisia that of a generous sibling or something else?

'Don't let her worry you,' Heidi said

aloud. 'Don't.'

Leaving the villa soon after, she met Rosa in the street outside the garden gate, walking down from the *gelateria* where she and Stefano were about to go to have an ice cream on that first day, before her true identity was discovered. Rosa smiled at her.

'Off to town to meet Gina?' she asked.

Heidi nodded, feeling guilty at maintaining the deception which had only been a spur of the moment act on her part, born of irritation at Marco's assumption that she would instantly agree to his every suggestion.

Rosa gave her a penetrating look. 'If you get bored with shopping, you might like to try the walk along the portico of San Luca to the hilltop sanctuary of the Madonna of San Luca. There are some wonderful views of the countryside from there.'

'Thank you, I'd like that,' Heidi said. 'In fact I'll suggest it. The walk might help to clear my head.'

She was surprised when Rosa touched

her arm. 'Are you still not well? Stefano was worried about you last night. He said you were very pale.'

'I'm fine.' Disconcerted by Rosa's genuine concern, Heidi was alarmed to find her eyes filling at the mention of Stefano. 'I'm just a little stale, I think. I need some exercise, get the blood pumping.'

'Of course.' Rosa looked uneasy at this idea but she politely agreed, adding, 'I hope you will like the sanctuary. It is very beautiful. Very holy and peaceful. It's a place of pilgrimage to the Madonna.'

'That sounds like just what I want,' Heidi said fervently.

* * *

From her guidebook, bought on her first day in Bologna, Heidi learned that the covered uphill walk from the city to the hilltop sanctuary of the Madonna of San Luca was the longest portico in the world. It was a popular place, but Heidi saw few people clambering the endless series of steps and slopes. Passing the florists, barbers, bars and ice cream parlors on the winding long portico's lower part, she felt the slope becoming steeper. Soon she was lengthening her stride and the secular shops gave way to religious frescoes and plaques recording the names of local dignitaries who had restored parts of the arcades.

She was trying to decide whether to remain with the family until this vital meeting about the future of Soleari's was over. Should she use her voting rights? Was she justified in doing so when she knew so little about the business? Perhaps she should tell Rosa this on her return from the sanctuary and then pack and leave. She would be lonely again, without family, but she was used to that.

'I am,' Heidi murmured, jogging defiantly up a few steps.

At first she thought the wail was her own sense of anguish perhaps bursting from her, then a police car down in the city. Stopping to listen, looking out over the grand houses and villas that were dotted here and there over the more open, hilly landscape outside Bologna, she heard it again — the exuberant swirl and drone of bagpipes.

'What?' Heidi began to chuckle with disbelief. Somewhere in one of those grand villa gardens someone was practicing the bagpipes. The sound made her want to both laugh and cry as a wave of homesickness broke over her. She had never felt more of a stranger and outsider than now, standing under one of the arcades listening to a haunting British folksong on bagpipes.

★ ★ ★

And that was how Stefano found her when he finally caught up after running most of the way from the start of the pilgrimage at the Saragozza gate. Mamma had told him where Heidi was going and had added that her young cousin had seemed pale and distracted.

'Heidi! Are you all right?' Stefano stopped, panting, beside a crumbling fresco. He thought she looked even worse than his mother had described — gray-faced, incredibly fragile. She was alone, too.

'Where's Gina?' he demanded, concern making his voice harsh.

'Gina couldn't make it.'

'Well, you can't possibly carry on as you are. Come back to the house.'

* * *

'Don't order me,' Heidi snapped. Any pleasure she'd had in seeing Stefano had vanished with his brusque greeting. 'I'm not your sister.'

The instant she spoke she regretted her words, but when Stefano remained silent and impassive, Heidi's own confusion and pain made her lash out at him again, determined to provoke some reaction.

'I'm leaving today. That should please you, Stefano. I know the only reason you've left Soleari's or wherever else you've been spending most of your time these days is because you're wondering how I'll vote. But I'm leaving, so you and Marco won't have to bother trying to charm me 'round. I won't be at your precious meeting. Now leave me alone!'

The bagpipes rose to another crescendo as Heidi stormed off, striding up the slope. Bells and chimes began to strike the hour throughout the city and then, closer, she heard steady breathing as Stefano easily caught up with her.

'You can't leave,' he said urgently. 'I don't want you to leave.'

'Oh, go back to Artemisia!' Heidi quickened her pace but could still not escape Stefano's reaching arms. The next moment, she found herself caught and, as she whirled about to demand that he release her, only succeeded in trapping her small, slim body against Stefano's taller, more muscled frame.

'Is that what you think?' Stefano asked quietly, as she jabbed her forearm against his middle.

'I'm not discussing anything while you man-handle me,' Heidi said, starting off again as Stefano instantly let her go.

He fell into step with her. 'Heidi, wait! Please! What are you talking about?'

'I would have thought that was obvious, but why not ask Marco? He was the one who thought I should know.'

'Marco told you that I was involved with my sister?' For an instant Stefano sounded disbelieving and then he cursed violently under his breath. 'Wait. No, stop.' He put an arm in front of her to prevent her moving forward. 'It's obvious that you know that I'm adopted, but you should know the rest.'

'Why didn't tell me you are adopted ? Didn't you trust me?'

'No! No, it was nothing like that.' A look of mingled pain and mortification slid across his face. 'I wasn't sure when to say anything. You seemed so pleased with the family that I hesitated to admit I was different. I wasn't sure what you'd think of me.' He sighed. 'I'm sorry.'

'And what about Artemisa?' Heidi flared up again, only slightly mollified by his halting explanation and recalling the silver bangle that she'd been shown by Artemisia only that morning. 'What does she think?'

Stefano's look of horror increased. 'Marco has a strong streak of mischief in his make-up. He knows that I think of Artemisia as my sister. She *is* my little sister by adoption, and for him to suggest I think of her otherwise ... It's disgraceful. I'm ashamed of him.'

He found her hand and gave it a gentle squeeze. 'Artemisia is currently involved with a millionaire who lives in Milan. That would be more her style, wouldn't you say?'

Heidi instantly thought that was it, but she was given no chance to reply. Stefano wrapped his arm around her waist and lifted her off her feet.

'Let's go home,' he said.

'And your gifts to her?' Heidi persisted, feeling a tingling delight in his arms but determined to find out, once and for all, about that silver bangle.

'Gifts?' Stefano's face cleared as he nodded understanding. 'Ah, you mean her present! Artemisia likes jewellery,

126

so I bought her a silver bracelet for her birthday. But that was months ago.'

His lips were brushing her forehead and when she did not protest, he lifted her higher in both arms to kiss her on the mouth.

'Stefano! This is a holy place!' Heidi protested when their long, sweet kiss had ended. 'Please, put me down. What if someone sees us?'

'I don't care,' Stefano said softly, kissing her again. He touched her hair and throat and shoulders with gentle fingers and then, as she struggled a little, playfully tightened his grip around her. 'Let's go home.'

* * *

At the end of the day Heidi sat up in bed hugging her knees, smiling as she remembered everything that she and Stefano had done. Once assured by her that she was really quite well, Stefano had told her that he'd taken a day off from the business that he wanted to spend with her. 'If that is acceptable to you,' he'd added anxiously.

Heidi had nodded, thinking of the contrast between his gallantry and Marco's arrogance and delighted at the prospect of spending so much time with him. He'd taken her sight-seeing around the city, going wherever she wanted to go, strolling with her round the colorful fruit and vegetable market, the bookshops, the massive cathedral of Saint Peter which, to her, looked more like a municipal building than a holy place, the Seven Churches and the church of San Dominico, where Saint Dominic was buried in an ornate marble tomb surrounded with tasseled incense burners and tall vases of white lilies.

That day at Heidi's request they had lunched at Luigi's, the café across the square from Soleari's where they had sat out of doors on the square under one of the café's colorful umbrellas and had cheerfully tried each other's dessert. Heidi had a spoonful of Stefano's spice cake, known by its local name of *certosino*, and she'd fed him a forkful of her own chocolate tartlet, moist with real chocolate and drenched with icing sugar.

'Working at Soleari's it's just as well for me that I never seem to put weight on.' Stefano patted his flat stomach. 'And you're obviously the same.' He leaned across the table and kissed Heidi on the cheek. 'My mother and sister are incredibly envious.'

Heidi smiled at him, no longer so self-conscious of the slight gap between her front teeth or her own slim shape, since Stefano seemed to find her pretty. Walking from Luigi's she'd been aware of admiring looks from other men and had felt astonishment and delight, although she thought that if she now realized she was reasonably attractive, it was because of the tall blond man striding beside her, who gave her confidence simply by his presence.

A lovely day, Heidi thought, wondering how many other such days there could be. What future realistically could she and Stefano have? In another ten days she would be returning to Britain, to her tiny flat in Selby and her aroma-therapy practice and lack of family. She had plenty of friends, but it was not the same. And would she see Stefano ever again?

Scared by that thought and misera-ble, Heidi laid back in bed, pulling the covers up tightly over her shoulders. Tonight at dinner, Artemisia had flirted outrageously with Stefano, compliment-ing him on his clothes, blowing him air kisses, and all the while, throwing Heidi searching glances, to see how she took it.

Artemisia can't help making a play for any man who's in the room with her, Heidi thought savagely, and then she was ashamed of her thought.

Marco meanwhile had been absent, and no one knew where he was. Heidi found Marco's behavior puzzling and malicious rather than Stefano's more generous interpretation of 'mischief', but perhaps her handsome relative saw her as a threat, especially if she decided to stay on for the family meeting about the future of Soleari's and used her voting rights. So far, she would vote for restoring the *panetteria* and not for any sale of the business and presumably Marco knew this.

Why could Marco not sort out his gambling debts? Heidi wondered. She remembered how Stefano had told her that in the past bread had been used to smuggle goods. A loaf would be hollowed out and a message or money or jewels placed inside, then a bread 'lid' would be replaced and the whole loaf repackaged. Was Marco perhaps involved in smuggling?

'Smuggling what?' Heidi scoffed aloud. She was allowing her imagination to go wild.

What was that? Heidi froze as she heard the door handle to her room being softly tried for a second time. Had she locked it? Should she put the light on and demand who was there. She drew in a soft breath, listening intently. She could hear nothing but the sound of the wind in the pine trees, but she sensed, with every taut nerve of her body, that someone was still lurking outside her door.

Thank goodness that she had locked it.

Still undecided whether to challenge whoever it was or simply to yell and wake the whole villa, Heidi heard a soft padding of footsteps moving away from the door and along the corridor.

Stark awake, she waited another half an hour before moving out of bed to jam a chair under the door handle and then returned shivering to her bed, where she did not sleep much for the rest of the night.

9

When she rose and dressed the following morning, Heidi was determined to act. She did not suspect Stefano of anything, but she had decided that she would not mention the incident to him alone. She wanted to catch the family together, confront them with what had happened and see how they reacted.

To her surprise, Rosa and Artemisia were already in the kitchen with Federico when she slipped downstairs. The big tiled kitchen, with its dark oak central table, was filled with the deliciously mingled scents of coffee, yeast and fresh bread — smells of family life, Heidi thought, the breath stopping in her throat. Soon she would have to leave this and Stefano, and the idea of tearing herself away made her want to rush weeping into the garden.

Someone had tried to enter her room last night, Heidi reminded herself.

Stiffened by this, she answered Artemisia's over-sweet, 'And how did you sleep, Heidi?' with a bracing, 'Excellently, thanks.'

'You do look much brighter this morning,' Rosa remarked, taking a sip of her espresso.

As do you, Heidi thought, smiling at her. Standing by the coffee maker, slim and elegant in another new tailored suit, this one in a flattering burgundy, Rosa was a different woman from the pale, apologetic figure Heidi had first met. Maybe I had some part in the change, Heidi comforted herself. If so, it perhaps went a small way to repay her debt to her relatives' generous hospitality.

'Little Heidi-Maria!' Marco came in behind her, pressing a button on his mobile phone before placing it on the oak table. 'You slept well, I trust?' This said while giving her his best movie star smile.

They were all in the kitchen now, everyone except Stefano, whom Heidi wanted to protect from this unpleasant mystery anyway. Smiling in return, Heidi admitted clearly, 'I would have slept better if whoever it was who tried my door last night had knocked first and had asked to come in. Was that you, Marco?'

'You were dreaming,' Artemisia scoffed, while Marco held up both hands.

'Not guilty!' he said. 'I never go where I'm not invited. Or were you hoping, perhaps, that I would?'

'Marco, you forget yourself,' said Federico sharply, turning from whatever he was doing by the oven to shake a finger at his youngest. 'Really!'

'Marco, please,' pleaded Rosa in a small voice.

'She was dreaming,' Artemisia repeated, her dark eyes flashing dislike.

'Oh, I'm sure that's what it was,' said Marco smoothly, registering Heidi's scalding blush with another wide smile. 'But these English girls, you know.'

'That's enough, Marco.'

Stefano stood framed in the open doorway leading to the garden. Marco took one look at his harsh, unyielding

135

face and was instantly silent as Stefano stalked into the kitchen. 'What's going on?' he demanded. 'Heidi, did I hear you correctly? Did you say that someone tried to enter your room last night?'

''Enter your room',' Artemisia mimicked. 'Don't be so stuffy. The silly girl was dreaming.'

'No, I wasn't!' snapped Heidi.

'Perhaps Stefano is so self-righteously indignant because he has a guilty conscience,' Marco went on, recovering fast and now offering a new, and to Heidi, an altogether more disturbing suggestion. 'You remember, Arte, how our Stefano used to sleep-walk around this house, especially after he'd told lies? I used to wonder if it was because he was afraid he might be sent back to the orphanage.'

'Marco, that's unfair!' Federico protested.

'Stefano hasn't sleep-walked for years,' Rosa said, her hands visibly shaking. She looked close to tears, and Heidi moved to comfort her.

'I used to sleep-walk as a child,' she said, praying that her face would not give away the fact that she was lying. After Marco's studied unkindness, she was determined to offer Stefano her public comfort and support. 'In fact that's why I lock my door at night,' she went on in seeming cheerfulness. 'So if that's all it was there's no harm done. Is there?'

Her question challenged both Marco and Artemisia, neither of whom replied.

★ ★ ★

She had tried to show Stefano support, but the incident saddened and embarrassed Heidi. After eating a small bread roll that she found almost impossible to swallow and drinking a hasty cup of tea that burned her mouth, she made an excuse and left the kitchen. Glad to be escaping the strained, frozen silence where none of the family were even glancing at each other, she decided to walk down into the city. She had no plans of where to go, but her absence might give Stefano and the others an opportunity to speak freely.

'I can't possibly stay on for the meeting,' Heidi murmured, opening the garden gate into the street. She was horrified by the tension and disruption that her presence had obviously provoked within the family. Whatever her hopes and feelings for Stefano, she couldn't remain at the villa. It would be selfish. It might not even be safe.

Why can't I fit in? The question haunted her as she pounded along the pavement, the more so because she knew that her dream of finding her father's family had in the end turned into both dream and nightmare.

'Heidi, wait for me.' Stefano caught her arm, and she swung round.

'What? Can't I go for a walk now?'

'Heidi, I'm sorry, really sorry about this morning. I should have told you about my sleepwalking, I know, but there's been no time and I honestly thought I hadn't done it for years. Years!'

Stefano stopped on the pavement in

front of her, his face racked with shame. Alarmed that he should blame himself when to her there was only one person who should feel guilty, Heidi put her arms around him.

'Did you really think Rosa and Federico would send you back to the orphanage?' she asked softly, hugging him as she felt a shudder run through his strong figure. 'I can understand that. For months after Papa died, I used to lie awake in bed listening for my grandparents. If I couldn't hear them I used to worry that they'd perhaps gone away in the night.'

'And left you. Oh, God, Heidi. My poor Heidi.' Stefano's arms were encircling her, hugging her tightly in return. Oblivious to the passing students and shoppers, they clung to each other.

* * *

Heidi glanced at her untouched ice cream and then stared out of the window of the *gelateria*, watching a man on an old black trike attached to a dustbin full of brooms and mops pedaling furiously uphill. She and Stefano were sitting in the ice cream parlor that he'd wanted to take her to on the first day they met. He had just been telling her about Gina, the youngest assistant at Soleari's, whom he'd escorted home first thing that morning after Gina had received a phone call in the *panetteria* and become very upset. Stefano had no idea who telephoned Gina or what the caller said, but Gina had been trembling and tearful. Stefano had swiftly taken her home, away from prying eyes and over-curious customers, but he had been uneasy about her ever since.

'I wish none of this was happening,' he said.

'If Gina's still upset tomorrow, perhaps I could help?' Heidi asked tentatively.

Stefano shook his head. 'I couldn't ask that of you, Heidi. That should be Marco's job, or Artemisia's. It wouldn't hurt them to work at the business for a change.' He frowned. 'I have to go away for a few days.'

Meeting Heidi's inquiring look, he took a deep breath and confessed, 'I have to leave Bologna this afternoon. I've a long-standing business meeting in Palermo in Sicily that I can't afford to break.'

This was a shock, and a bitter blow to Heidi, but she determined not to add to Stefano's problems by showing how upset she was. 'How long will you be gone?' she asked, pushing her ice cream to one side across the tiled table.

'Two, three days. No longer than that, I promise. Why not take the opportunity to have a change yourself? Stay at a local hotel in Bologna and pamper yourself. I'll pay.' The sudden brightness in his face faded as Heidi shook her head.

'I'll be perfectly all right at the villa,' she told him gently, telling herself she was only slightly hurt that he had not invited her to go with him.

'But someone tried your door last night! Marco says it must have been me sleepwalking, but I'm sure it wasn't. So, who was it?' Stefano struck his palm on the table for emphasis, rattling their empty cappuccino cups. 'Stay at a hotel. I'll pay,' he repeated.

'I'm not letting Rosa down by making her feel I don't trust her family. I can take care of myself.' Heidi gave a teasing grin when Stefano looked as if he would argue again. 'Don't you trust me?'

'Of course I do,' he said. 'But you *will* be careful?'

'I will,' Heidi promised. She was horribly disappointed that Stefano was leaving but perversely glad of his anxious concern for her. He'd not said anything about his feelings, but surely he cared a little for her? Why else would he worry?

Perhaps because of your voting rights, a nasty inner voice reminded her; a voice she resolutely ignored.

★   ★   ★

That night, with Stefano gone, Heidi did not expect to sleep, but when she next opened her eyes on a beautiful dawn morning, she felt as relaxed and refreshed as if she had treated herself to aromatherapy. Marco and Artemisia were both missing at breakfast, and when Rosa hesitantly asked her if she minded doing a little shopping, Heidi was happy to oblige.

'Will you be home for lunch?' Rosa asked.

'No, thanks. I'll pick something up while I'm out,' Heidi said easily. She had her own plans, and since these involved Soleari's, she decided not to mention anything to Rosa or to anyone else. She wanted to take another look at the *panetteria*, partly to savor that delicious window display, partly to reassure herself that there had been no more incidents of sabotage.

Rosa's shopping took longer than Heidi expected, but only because she found the people and the colorful market stalls and the arcaded Bologna streets endlessly fascinating. Pausing to admire an old religious fresco at one of the street corners, she realized with a start of surprise that it was mid-afternoon and the shops were closing for the siesta. She could hear the sound of clinking knives and forks from the shuttered first floor apartments of the Renaissance buildings she was passing, and the only creature moving across the small square ahead was a feral, fawn-colored cat.

A cat and now a stocky, gray-haired figure with a red rose buttonhole, striding with a bustling purpose she knew well. Her cousin Federico, obviously going somewhere.

'It's Thursday,' Heidi breathed, as she set off after him. She knew she shouldn't follow, that what the poor man did on Thursday afternoons was nothing to do with her, but curiosity won out over guilt. Why not? she thought, stealing after Federico across the square as lightly as the cat. No one need ever know.

Another street and another row of terracotta-colored apartments, with iron bars across the shuttered windows on the ground floor and walls covered in political posters. Federico pressed the door pad beside one of the anonymous, paint-peeling doors and after a few moments, was allowed inside.

Heidi hurried to read the names on the door pad and almost laughed out loud when she realized where he had gone. There was only one name on the door pad, written in fine calligraphy.

'Studio Fra Lippo Lippi — Learn to paint like a master!' she read aloud. So this was Federico's grand passion! Not another woman but art classes.

The door to the studio clicked open, and with a definite twinkle in his crinkled brown eyes, Federico beckoned her inside. 'And now that you've tracked me down, niece, you might as well know the rest.'

* * *

The studio was large and airy and full of students of all ages at a drawing class. Federico showed her his easel and regular workspace and then, with permission

145

from the tutor, brought Heidi to a smaller room whose walls were gradually being filled with pictures.

'For our summer exhibition,' Federico told her proudly. 'Here's my section of wall.'

There, hanging in pride of place, was a newly-finished portrait of a softly-idealized Rosa, sitting on a wicker chair holding a posy of pink roses.

'I've painted it for her birthday in August,' Federico explained. 'Do you think she'll like it? Do you think it does her justice?'

Heidi smiled. 'I think she'll love it,' she said.

'Rosa is very fond of you, Heidi. She says you've made a real difference to her life.' As Heidi blushed at this lavish praise, Federico patted her arm. 'For me, having you here is like having Ruggiero back. Marco and Artemisia will see that, too. You just need to give them time.

'It's strange, really,' Federico continued. 'I'm the one who wants to learn to paint, but it's Artemisia who has the talent. She has a real eye for shape and color, you know, so you'd expect it would be her who'd be responsible for the packaging side of the business. But Marco wanted it, and since he's a real whiz with computers and graphics, he got it.'

'Do you like his designs?' Heidi asked.

Federico shrugged. 'Call me an old traditional baker, but sometimes I think his stuff is a bit too way-out. Still, it's what's inside the cake and bread boxes that matters, and Stefano handles that.'

'Does Marco resent that?' Heidi asked carefully.

'Marco? No! He doesn't want to get up at three in the morning to bake every day!'

10

Thinking back to their conversation as she battled through the afternoon heat to reach Soleari's before it closed for the siesta, Heidi wondered what Federico and Rosa would make of Marco's extensive gambling debts, if they knew of them. With the late spring sun scorching the back of her neck, she sped along the main square, avoiding the cars and mopeds. Bologna's last two remaining medieval towers loomed above the Palazzo Del Podesta and emotion rose in her throat as she saw the names and photographs of the resistance victims on the memorial plaque in the square. Slowing to read more, she realized in horror that in one tragic case five brothers from the same family had perished in the Second World War.

Perhaps it was because she was standing so still and quiet that the men's laughter issuing from a nearby arcade seemed brazen, almost callous. Glaring across the square at them, Heidi gasped and shaded her eyes, convinced she must be mistaken.

But she was not wrong, and Heidi knew it as she whirled about on the spot, turning her back on the two men and walking swiftly into the sheltering shade of the nearest tall building. She did not stop until she had turned a corner, and there, she leaned against the peeling ochre-painted wall and tried to collect her shattered wits. Although now in shade, she felt clammy and feverish as disbelieving tears pricked at her eyes.

She could not ignore what she'd seen and now she admitted it. One of the men laughing on the edge of the square had been Stefano. 'He said he'd be in Palermo,' Heidi mumbled through trembling lips. 'Perhaps he was able to come back early.'

But she couldn't quite believe that, or rather it seemed naive to do so. The simple facts of geography, distance and times of air travel were against that idea. Much more likely was the shocking thought that Stefano had never left Bologna, that he'd deliberately deceived her, and the rest of the family, and his own loyal employees at Soleari's.

Why should he do that? Heidi asked herself desperately, as other questions crowded her mind. Who was the man he was with? Why was he not in Palermo?

Harder than the questions was her own sense of disillusionment. She had believed Stefano when he told her about Soleari's and what he thought was best for the future of the *panetteria*. But had he told her everything? Had he told her the truth? Did he perhaps want to keep Soleari's frozen in time and small-scale not to preserve the excellence of its bread and fresh hand-made pasta but for more sinister reasons?

Thinking furiously, Heidi raced across the path of an accelerating scooter to dart along another arcaded street, ignoring the scooter driver's furious volley of curses. Perhaps for 'special customers' Stefano provided prettily-wrapped bread and cakes with missing centers that held drugs or other illegal items. Who would suspect a family bakery?

It's Marco who likes the good life, Heidi argued with herself, but it was Stefano who wanted to keep the business as it was, not Marco. Over and over, in her mind she replayed the sight of his distinctive blond hair and the sound of his laughter ringing across the square until she felt that he was laughing at her. How could she have ever imagined that they were close? In truth, she hardly knew Stefano, knew nothing of the possibly illegal acts he might be capable of, once pressed. He had not even told her of his adoption until forced to do so by others. A snippet of Marco's conversation with her in the restaurant at Roberto's drifted back into her memory, 'He's very competitive. Stefano likes to win at everything he does.' What if Marco was right, and Stefano had been sleepwalking because he had lied?

'That's absurd,' Heidi told herself, but she did not feel reassured. Clutching her shopping bags tighter, she quickened her pace even more. Soleari's itself should hold the answer to her questions, she thought, but she must reach it before it closed.

★ ★ ★

Gina, the youngest assistant, was closing the shutters on the window display at Soleari's when Heidi crossed the square. A plump, cheerful young woman, Gina's usually glowing complexion looked blotchy and her brown hair seemed to have lost its natural chestnut highlights. Her white chef's uniform was as spotless as ever but she moved with none of her usual bounce. Greeting her and asking how she was, Heidi inwardly prayed that nothing had happened to Gina's fiancée, that the wedding was still on.

'I'm fine,' Gina said, careful not to look at Heidi directly. 'Everything's fine now.'

Even as she spoke, tears sprang into her eyes. 'I'm just tired,' she murmured.

'What is it, Gina?' Heidi asked softly. She dropped her shopping bags onto the floor, leaving them where they lay, and approached her.

'Nothing.' Gina began to tremble.

'I know you were upset after your phone call yesterday. Can I help you now?' Heidi went on, gently shepherding Gina through the door and away from the few remaining customers who lingered along the shady pavement outside.

'No, it's nothing.' Gina's pretty face twisted in her effort not to cry, and Heidi felt dreadful at having provoked this response. But then Gina leaned into her sheltering arm and added in an urgent whisper, 'I must talk to you!'

'Come on,' Heidi encouraged. 'Let's find somewhere private.'

Swiftly, she drew Gina through the shop, past Alberto who was wiping down shelves, moving at a smart pace towards the ladies' cloakroom.

'Emilia will be putting on her make-up in the rest room!' Gina warned, her breath catching as she fought down sobs.

She was on the verge of tears.

'This way!' Heidi pointed to the stair-case. Beside her, Gina was now openly weeping, trying to mop her streaming eyes with a tissue. Climbing the stairs, Heidi turned out her pockets until she found a clean handkerchief. 'Here.' She handed it across before pushing open the door to the staff lunch room where, only recently, she and Stefano had so enjoyed each others' company.

Except that it wasn't the staff room. By mistake she had brought them to an office with two large desks and comput-ers and, standing beneath the window and its closed blinds, a water cooler.

'Sit down a moment, catch your breath.' Heidi gave Gina a brief hug before releasing her, longing to tell her that it would be all right but hardly daring to speak in case she made things worse. Was poor Gina distraught because of a lovers' quarrel, or a family tragedy, or was it, as Heidi increasingly suspected, something to do with the place where she worked?

She fetched Gina a glass of water and made a deliberate act of walking slowly around the two desks, giving her companion time to compose herself. Both desks were modern, in a simple Swedish-style design, and with no distinguishing marks. The computers on these desks were similarly anonymous, without so much as a single sticker or cuddly toy.

Beside the desk with a large swivel chair, Heidi's attention was drawn to a scrap of print-out paper in the nearby waste bin. She was alerted chiefly by the faint charred scent, because the paper was badly scorched. Crouching to examine the print-out, she made out the word 'difficulties' and then there was a gap where the paper had completely burned away, and then 'enable a sexier offer,' and, after another gap in the scorched paper, 'worthwhile'.

You shouldn't be looking, Heidi's conscience scolded, but her curiosity was stronger. Glancing up from the waste bin, she noticed a handsome print of

Botticelli's *La Primavera* hanging on the wall immediately opposite the other desk. She remembered Artemisia's scornful comment, 'Soleari's isn't just a bakery. It's not a 'bread shop' . . . that's like calling a painting by Botticelli a daub.' Was the desk opposite the Botticelli's painting of Spring-time Artemisia's? If so, to whom did this second desk belong? It's very plainness made Heidi wonder if it was Stefano's, which quenched her spirits further, since presumably Stefano had been the one who had received and then burned the email print-out mentioning 'a sexier offer'.

Sitting on a spare chair, Gina finished her water and began to talk. 'It started a couple of weeks ago as a joke,' she said, her voice hesitant at first, becoming stronger as Heidi said encouragingly, 'Go on.'

'I did something silly with one of the oven timers. I won't bother trying to explain what because that isn't important. What matters is that he suggested it as a joke, and I did as he asked because

I thought it would be amusing.'

'And it wasn't?'

'No!' Gina began to sniffle again.

'Who asked you?' Heidi prompted, when Gina fell silent. 'Who was it, Gina?'

Gina took in a long breath and clutched her empty water glass more tightly. 'He wanted me to do it again with the oven. I told him no, that it hadn't been that funny, but he said that I should do as he said because otherwise he would tell everyone else — Alberto, Emilia, everyone. He said I'd lose my job. And I love my work, I really do.' Gina began to cry again, very quietly.

'But who told you to do these things?' Heidi asked again. A name rose slowly and hotly in her throat, threatening to choke her, but she forced herself to say it. 'Stefano?'

Gina broke down completely, sobbing so loudly that Heidi could hardly hear, much less understand what she was saying. She caught the words 'shame' and 'sorry,' before Gina gasped out, 'He . . . he does not like it when people say no to him.

'After a batch of olive focaccie were burned to a crisp and then old Signor Bartoli almost fell into the cellar, I became really scared,' she went on, wiping her eyes with Heidi's handkerchief. 'That open trapdoor certainly wasn't me. It must have been another of his people, but I guessed who was behind it. I refused to have anything to do with him.'

'That's good, Gina, but you must tell me his name.' Heidi could not believe it was Stefano who had bullied and threatened in this way — she was desperate not to believe it.

'Who is pressurizing you? And did he telephone and threaten you yesterday?'

Gina nodded and began to rock to and fro on the chair. Her heart full of pity, Heidi walked across to the young woman and knelt beside her.

'Gina, it will be all right. You're not going to lose your job for something that you did as a joke, but you'll have to come clean and admit what happened. Otherwise this man, whoever he is, will keep on blackmailing you.'

Could Stefano really be doing this? Surely that was impossible!

'No, no!' Gina wailed now. 'I can't say anything! I can't afford to lose my job, especially now. My wedding dress cost over two thousand euros!'

'Let me help you,' Heidi pleaded. 'I'll talk to the others, but you have to tell me. Gina, who is it?'

Behind her, she heard the rapid footsteps on the stairs. Straightening quickly and placing herself between the opening door and the sobbing Gina, Heidi prepared to meet whoever was coming into the office.

11

Marco strolled into the room, glanced at Gina and said easily, 'Hello, Heidi-Maria, I see Gina has been telling you about Stefano.' He smiled and then added in a more serious tone, 'Do you understand now? Stefano will do anything to keep Soleari's in the dark ages. Isn't that so, Gina?'

Heidi stared with horror as Gina nodded her head. 'But that would mean —' Heidi stopped as her stomach turned over within her. Gina had just been telling her about the mysterious 'him' who had threatened and blackmailed her. Now Marco was suggesting that 'him' was Stefano, and Gina had agreed!

Gina, threatened by Stefano? Stefano, harming his own people? Did Gina really mean that?

It isn't possible, Heidi thought. She felt stunned with disbelief. This was worse than incredible. It was a living nightmare. Stefano had told her nothing about himself, not one story of the time he spent in the orphanage or if he remembered his natural parents. Why did he not want to share? Now he was lying to her, telling her he'd be in Palermo when all the while he was here in the city, bullying Gina. It was a horrifying, sickening betrayal of trust.

What do you expect? drawled a voice in her mind that sounded eerily like Marco's. *He's the adopted son. He's not one of us by blood.*

I don't believe that nonsense, Heidi thought, and she rallied. Stefano would tell her more when he was not beset by problems, when they had more time to relax together. For an instant she had been thrown off-balance by these seeming 'revelations', but how real were they? Gina was still distressed, ready to agree with any stronger personality, so of what value was her account?

But she was losing concentration and her grasp on events. Marco was talking, and she'd better pay attention.

Leaning against the desk opposite the reproduction of the Botticelli painting, Marco was holding forth, clearly enjoying this moment.

'Yes, and if our potential buyers learned about the troubles at Soleari's they might easily pull out.' He smiled at Gina, who seemed rooted to her chair.

'Or demand the business for a cheaper price?' Heidi dropped in, determined to put forth an opposing point of view.

Marco waved aside her objection. 'Unlikely,' he said. 'That might happen in Britain, but not here. In Italy, we do business properly. A solid reputation is everything. Stefano clearly hoped to undermine our reputation so that our buyers would vanish away like mist.'

Inwardly raging at that insult about Britain, Heidi rearranged her face into what she hoped was a convinced expression. 'That's terrible.' She reached out and gave Gina a comforting squeeze on the shoulder. Gina had stopped crying in the last few moments, but she was still upset. 'Can I telephone anyone for you?'

Heidi asked her gently, thinking that Gina might welcome the appearance of her boyfriend.

'No, I'll be all right.' Gina rose to her feet and tottered to the door, saying without looking at either Heidi or Marco, 'I'll see if Alberto and Emilia need help clearing up.'

She was gone, and Heidi was glad to hear Gina's footsteps heading safely downstairs. 'So what now?' she asked, speaking to Marco but really addressing herself. Stefano, a liar and a blackmailer? She could not bear to think of him in those terms. Had she been mistaken about him? Could she have fallen in love with such a man?

Staring after Gina, a fleeing figure in white, Marco said quickly, 'I realize this has been a huge shock for you, Heidi. I know you liked Stefano, and I'm sure you won't want to run into him again, not on this trip, at least.'

Heidi was silently staggered at Marco's glib assessment of her feelings and also of her character. She very much wanted to talk to Stefano, to give him the chance to explain what he had done and why. Why was he here today in Bologna, when he had told her — and the family — that he would be in Palermo?

'It's probably best if you leave quietly today, while Stefano is away. It's obvious that he's an obsessive sort of character, possibly even dangerous.' Speaking, Marco held the office door open for her to go first. 'I've got my car nearby, so I can take you back to the villa and you can pack, say your farewells and then I can drive you to the station or wherever you want to go.'

Marco was trying to rush her, wanting to hustle her off. Heidi was already aware that he didn't want her at the rapidly approaching family meeting, where the future of Soleari's would be decided by vote, but she wondered at his haste today.

Why don't you want me to talk to Stefano? she questioned him in her mind as she walked down the staircase and back into the panetteria. Noting the muted greetings that Emilia and Alberto gave Marco, she found herself asking why Gina had seemed to freeze like a rabbit in the headlights of a car whenever Marco smiled at her.

Still dazed by Marco's claims, Heidi turned and waited for her handsome cousin to catch up. He was talking quietly to Gina, he smiling, Gina nodding. Waiting again, Heidi could not help thinking about Stefano. Her sense of him was very strong here, amidst the glass shelves and small tables with their displays of cake boxes and streamer-trimmed bags of fresh pasta.

In a series of frozen tableaux in her mind, she remembered him. How sensitive and concerned Stefano had been on her first night in the villa, when Federico had cavalierly cancelled her hotel room and Stefano had instantly stepped forward to help, offering to drive her back to the hotel. She remembered him brushing her hair and how careful and gentle he'd been. He had come rushing up the longest portico in the world, over half the length of the covered four kilometer uphill walk from the city to the hilltop sanctuary of the Madonna of San Luca because he'd been worried about her. She remembered the tender urgency of his kisses.

Stefano had shown her nothing but good. She remembered him with others, too, his saving of Signor Bartoli; his indulgence of Emilia's teasing; his protectiveness towards Rosa. He had escorted Gina home because she was upset. Was it really believable, Heidi thought, that Stefano had been the one to upset her?

I trust him, she thought. Despite the dreadful shock of seeing him in town today, she still trusted Stefano. In contrast, and in a basic, fundamental way, Heidi realized that she could not trust Marco at all. On the heels of that realization came another, that it would not be prudent to get into Marco's car.

What had Gina said? 'He does not like it when people say no to him.' Did that description not fit Marco, the spoiled younger son, absolutely?

As she left Soleari's, she wordlessly practiced what she would say and do. On the pavement outside, she spoke to Marco, her voice light. 'I'm sorry, Marco, but I need to go to the chemist's. It'll be quicker if I walk. It's right in the middle of town, by the food market.' She was backing slowly away as she spoke. 'I'll see you back at the villa, okay?'

Marco was following her. He was smiling but silent, matching his steps to hers, as if they were involved in some kind of dance. A shiver of fear iced its way down Heidi's back as she watched this tall, good looking man prowling after her in his designer jeans and black cotton-silk shirt.

He does not like it when people say no to him . . .

'I have to go.' Heidi knew she was still backing away along the arcade, but she wasn't too proud to admit that she was scared to turn her back on Marco. Her hesitant feet found the edge of the pavement at the end of the square, and she knew that before she moved further, she had to find a means to distract him.

'Look!' She pointed behind Marco's shoulder towards Luigi's café, forcing her taut mouth into a large smile. 'Isn't that . . . Hey! Hello!' she called out.

Marco turned, and Heidi was off, walking quickly down the pavement, across the narrow street at the end of the square and then immediately a hard right down another alleyway. Her light sandals pounding the hard flagstones, she ran, skirting wildly around a parked Mercedes that filled most of the alley, ignoring any raised voices or the usual car horns and building drills that were so much a part of the daily sounds of Bologna. Tasting the salt of tears in her mouth, she ran on, allowing the prevailing wind to blow her along the street like a piece of thistledown.

Careering into a new alleyway, narrowly missing a startled-looking woman pushing two toddlers in smocked gingham dresses in a double buggy, Heidi pushed herself to go faster, faster.

Missing her footing once, her legs

scissored widely and she tumbled, a cry escaping from her as she realized she was falling.

Strong arms caught her, and she screamed, shuddering from head to foot, terrified for an instant that Marco had seized her.

'It's all right,' Stefano said softly against her ear, easily supporting her as her legs buckled. 'I won't let you fall. It's all right, my Heidi. I can explain.'

'Well done, Stefano. You do have this irritating knack of being in the way.' Marco, breathing heavily, stepped up to his taller, leaner brother and chuckled as Heidi turned her face away from his, resting her head in the crook of Stefano's shielding arm. 'That wasn't very well-mannered, Heidi-Maria, rushing off like that. Now, why don't you come away from him?'

Marco made a grab for her, but even as Heidi shied away, Stefano had turned his own body so that Marco's reaching fingers scraped down his shoulder and arm and did not touch her.

'Let me go!' Heidi whispered, disliking the feeling of being trapped between the two brothers, one very fair, one very dark, one she could trust, one she was increasingly afraid of.

Glowering at Marco, Stefano instantly released her. For Heidi, his immediate acknowledgement of her wishes provided the final proof of both her hopes and her darkest suspicions. Realizing the truth, she gasped as everything else fell into place.

Marco gave a rueful grin at her reaction. 'It's over,' he drawled, addressing Stefano over her head. 'You've been found out, Stefano. And why aren't you in Palermo, as you told us? You do realize that Heidi has been incredibly disappointed and —'

'You were the one behind the sabotage,' Heidi interrupted him. Sensing that here and now would see a final confrontation, she stepped forward to face Marco. 'Do you deny it?'

She glanced at Stefano. 'Is that what you suspected? Did you allow us to think you were away so that you could watch Soleari's and finally see how Marco was bullying and blackmailing Gina and others into doing his dirty work for him?'

'That's absurd.' Marco smilingly denied it, tapping the side of his head with a finger. 'I think you've had rather too much sun again, Heidi-Maria.'

'And in the office, that was your desk,' Heidi continued, throwing Stefano a glance of apology for ever suspecting him. Of course the desk near the Botticelli print was Artemisia's and the completely plain desk was Marco's. He was hardly ever there to add any personal touches. If the desk was Marco's, then the half-burned contents of the waste bin were his, too.

'I saw you at breakfast with your mobile,' Heidi countered, more and more convinced that what she was saying was right. 'You'd just finished a call to Gina, hadn't you? She's afraid of you. That's why she agreed with you upstairs in the staff office when you said it was your brother who was organizing those 'accidents' in the bakery.'

Marco put up his hands. '*Panetteria*, please,' he said.

'You were working at the *panetteria*, arranging that 'wizard bread' display when Nix was taken ill with one of Soleari's vol-au-vents,' Heidi said, part of her deeply relieved now that she understood that Stefano had played no part in poisoning the little dog.

'Nix? Who on earth is that?' Marco blustered, but Heidi cut across him.

'Soleari's is very busy. There are always people milling around the counters. It would have been easy for you to spike part of Signora Cardenli's order.'

'And alter the timers,' broke in Stefano, his face hardening. 'But why? I really hoped I was mistaken in my suspicions of you, and I kept hoping I was wrong, but I wasn't. But why Marco? Why do this?'

Marco shrugged and refused to answer, brushing a speck of ochre paint off his black shirt and glancing hopefully to the end of the alleyway as a Vespa trundled across the top of the street from one arcade to another. When the driver did not turn down towards them, he smirked and turned back to Heidi. 'Are you going to say next that it was me who tried your door a couple of nights ago? Believe me, you're not so attractive —'

Stefano cursed and shot across the cobbles towards his brother, but Heidi grabbed his arm. 'Don't!' she said urgently. 'It doesn't matter. He didn't hurt me, and he only did it to encourage me to leave the Villa Rosa before the family meeting.'

Marco sighed and straightened as he realized that Stefano was not going to launch himself at him. 'Excellent thought. Pity you didn't act on it.'

'But you've acted, haven't you?' Heidi went on. 'You went so far as to have someone open that trap-door and leave it. Did you tell whoever did that for you that it was for a joke, as you told Gina? Were you hoping to obtain a more competitive price for the *panetteria* for its potential buyers? Were they going to make it more 'worthwhile' for you if you could give them the chance to present 'a sexier offer'?'

She hurled the terms of the mystery email printout back at Marco. Beside her, standing in the middle of the narrow alley as if in defiance of any passing moped and Vespa drivers, Stefano looked coldly furious at the revelation of his brother's treatment of Gina, then puzzled.

'Sexier offer?' he repeated. 'You mean you did this for money?' he asked Marco, his bright brown eyes shining with pain and confusion. 'Simply for money? I'd hoped I was mistaken, that the odd hints Gina gave me that made me dread it might be you behind these 'accidents' were going to turn out to be groundless. Marco, why couldn't you have come to me for help? Or to Artemisia? We wouldn't have stood by and let you sink under a mountain of debt. You only had to ask.'

'Give you another chance to play patronizing older brother? No way. As for Arte . . .' Marco snapped his fingers so hard that Heidi flinched. 'She's bailed me out twice but no more. Why does this pathetic little *panetteria* mean so much to you, anyway? My scheme would have seen us all rich.'

Stefano clenched his fists by his sides. 'What about the tradition? The people like Alberto who've served us faithfully over the years? The pleasure and joy we bring to others, the pride in our work, in what we produce. Do these things mean nothing to you?'

Marco said quietly, 'You're wrong. You're both making a huge mistake, but I suppose that's your privilege.' He turned in the street, just as a moped driver skidded round the corner and bore down on them, blowing her horn as she swerved around Stefano. 'I'll see you around, maybe.'

With a wave and a final dazzling smile, Marco was gone, striding off in the same direction as the moped driver. Building shadows hid his tall, black-shirted figure and then, a few moments later, Heidi heard the roar of a car pulling away in a screech of tires. Torn between relief and a kind of shocked numbness, she leaned back against the alley wall, feeling the chill bite of metal against her shoulder from one of the building's iron window grilles. Silent and still, she and Stefano stared at each other, feeling no sense of satisfaction at their unraveling of the mysterious 'accidents' at Soleari's, but only a resigned sadness.

★ ★ ★

Finally, Stefano crossed the narrow alleyway out of the path of passing mopeds, joining Heidi in leaning against the alley wall as he took off his spectacles and gave them a long polish on his jeans.

'I'm sorry,' he said, looking at Heidi without his glasses, his gaze holding hers. 'I deceived you, and I shouldn't have done. I was trying to keep you out of danger, but instead I brought you closer to it.'

Heidi shook her head. 'No, you

didn't,' she said, reaching out and clasping his arm as he put on his spectacles. 'But you should have told me what you were doing. When I spotted you today in Bologna I wondered if I was seeing you or your double.'

Staring up at him, she had the rare experience of seeing Stefano visibly discomforted, the more so as a slow blush swept over his face.

'I wanted to keep you out of it,' he growled. 'You're the last person to stay on the sidelines if there's trouble, and I didn't want you involved.'

Heidi refused to be distracted by Stefano's implied compliment, if compliment it was. 'Who was the man you were laughing with today, close to the Palazzo Del Podesta? And for how long have you suspected Marco?' she asked gently, reluctant to pry but sensing that these hard questions must be settled between them.

Stefano smiled at her as a troop of elderly Italian tourists walked slowly past them, led by their gesturing guide.

'Would you believe that man was a policeman?' he told her under cover of the tourists' shuffling footsteps. 'He's an old school friend whom I joined at one of the local bars for a drink. I was chatting to him about his surveillance work, trying to draw him out about clues and signs when you must have spotted us. I suppose I was thinking I'd be my own detective.' He sighed. 'When the 'accidents' first started, I wondered about Marco and remembered how he loved to play tricks when he was a little boy. But then I told myself he was an adult, that he would not be so petty. I suppose I did not want to think of my brother in that way.

'I didn't tell my friend Pietro anything about Soleari's, or what I was afraid might be happening there. It would have sounded too bizarre. I was too ashamed.' He lowered his head.

That was Marco's talent, Heidi thought, his ability to make members of his own family feel guilty. Impulsively, she touched Stefano's arm. 'It's not your fault.'

Stefano ran a distracted hand through his wavy blond hair. 'I knew Marco had the strongest reasons for wanting the business sold, but I didn't want to believe that he would actually sabotage it. Gina was white and trembling when I took her home after that phone call. As I said earlier, the little she would tell me about her mystery caller made me think of Marco again, made me determined to stop him, to unmask his filthy campaign of dirty tricks. And then there was his treatment of you.'

'Me?'

'His insolence, his unkindness.' Stefano folded his wiry arms across his chest, tightly gripping his elbows. 'I was so jealous of Marco when he took you out to Roberto's restaurant and asked you to go to Venice with him. So jealous and so afraid that you'd fall for his easy charm.'

'I suppose women usually do?' Heidi asked, thinking that this explained Marco's invitations. He'd been trying to charm her into doing whatever he wanted, especially with regard to the family business.

'Usually, damn him!' Stefano kicked the wall with the back of his heel. 'And there you were, so pretty, and second cousin to him, nothing to stop you both . . .' His voice trailed away and he would not look directly at her.

So here was the reason Stefano had been so brusque with her whenever he'd seen her with Marco! Heidi's hopes and spirits began to lift, to almost soar. Jealousy was not the result of indifference, or caring solely about how she used her voting rights. 'He is good looking,' she said in a considering way, 'But we're not really suited. We don't have anything in common and I'm pretty serious.'

Stefano unfolded his arms. 'That's what Artemisia is always saying about me,' he said, his voice tense with barely suppressed emotion.

'Serious and caring,' Heidi agreed. *And with hair as golden as the bread you bake and wonderful warm brown eyes*, she added in her mind, too shy to speak her thought aloud.

Perhaps something of her feeling showed in her face because the next moment she was in Stefano's arms, being whirled off her feet.

'Lord, Heidi, I've been so worried about you!' he exclaimed, lifting her high in his arms, oblivious to a passing disapproving priest. 'When you cannoned into me today, you looked so pale, so scared. I went through hell, wondering what was wrong, what had happened to you. When Marco came after you, I wanted to kill him.'

'I'm all right,' Heidi swiftly reassured him as his arms tightened around her waist. She felt to be floating away, buoyed up by his concern. 'Nothing happened, Stefano. I was never in any danger.' She said nothing of her sudden reluctance to go with Marco in his car. Stefano, she sensed, had already been badly torn by family loyalties and family responsibilities because of his younger brother. Trying to keep it light, she asked quizzically, 'Are you always this protective?'

Stefano gave her a long kiss that made her feel even more light-headed. 'Of you, my Heidi? Oh, yes,' he said, kissing her again as he set her down gently on her feet. 'I like to look after you.'

'Isn't that rather old-fashioned?' Heidi teased as they turned and began to walk hand in hand back towards Soleari's, their family business.

'Maybe.' Stefano swung her hand up to his lips and kissed her fingers one by one. 'I don't care.'

Neither do I, Heidi thought, as they strolled into the sunlit square. Above her head and around her, she could hear bells ringing, a joyous sound, driving away the last of the shadows that had hemmed them both in since Marco had tried to set his devious plans in motion.

'I wonder if we'll see Marco at home,' she said aloud.

'That's unlikely. My brother likes to avoid reckonings if he can. I imagine he'll be on his way to Milan or farther.

We'll probably hear from him in a few days' time.' Stefano gently squeezed her hand. 'I know you care for all the family and your coming amongst us has certainly transformed my mother's life, but you really mustn't worry about Marco. He always lands on his feet.'

'Even with his gambling debts?'

'Even with those,' Stefano answered.

★ ★ ★

Stefano was right. When he and Heidi returned to the Villa Rosa later that afternoon, Marco was nowhere to be found. A few days' later, on the morning of the family meeting to consider the future of Soleari's, Marco emailed a proxy vote to Artemisia with the instruction to, 'Do exactly what you want with it.'

Stefano insisted that the meeting take place at Soleari's, in the staff lunch room next to the plain office. There, within the sounds and mouthwatering smells of the *panetteria*, Stefano explained how the ovens need to be repaired and modernized and for long how the business would have to close while this work went on. Federico and Rosa sat side by side, holding hands as they listened to his intense, careful account.

Watching them together and seeing Rosa's increased aura of peace and serenity, Heidi wondered if Federico had decided to show his wife the birthday portrait he had made for her a little early. Rosa glowed with life.

'What's wrong with you two?' Artemisia snapped, as Federico and Rosa smiled through her presentation about the advantages of selling Soleari's. 'We could make a great deal of money here, and you're hardly listening to a word I'm saying!'

'Money isn't everything, is it?' observed Federico, nodding to Stefano across the table. 'I think it's time we voted.'

Heidi voted with Stefano to restore the *panetteria*, but she was glad that her vote was not needed. Rosa and Federico both voted with their adopted son, and

Federico even used his casting vote on that side. Faced with a five to two split, Artemisia took the result in surprisingly good part, saying that she wasn't entirely surprised and that neither was Marco.

'In fact he told me to tell you that he's giving up his share and interest in the business,' Artemisia announced, with the air of a cat with a freshly-captured mouse. 'He's going to devote himself to his new wife-to-be, the Contessa Donna Maria Eugenia of Palermo. They met recently in Milan and are going to announce their engagement this weekend.'

'See what I mean?' Stefano remarked in a low voice to Heidi as Rosa and Federico broke into starts and exclamations of mingled surprise and delight. 'Marco always lands on his feet.'

* * *

Later, Heidi and Stefano slipped away into the garden of the Villa Rosa to walk and talk. Heidi was returning to Britain in two days' time to pick up her old life. Strolling along the terraces towards the small fountain where Stefano had first kissed her, she realized that the thought gave her scarcely any pleasure. Stefano had said that she had transformed Rosa's life. Federico had told her that having her around was like having his brother Ruggiero back. The staff and increasingly the customers at Soleari's greeted her as one of their own. She would be leaving all that behind, leaving this new family, leaving Stefano.

Had she transformed Stefano's life? she thought, stealing a glance at his reserved, aristocratic-looking profile as they wandered side by side along an avenue of ferns and pines. Would he be able to return to Soleari's in three days' time with no more than a few memories and perhaps the odd regret? Was their brief time together to be no more than a holiday romance?

'I will write to you,' Stefano suddenly announced. 'Every day.'

'It will be nice to keep in touch.' *Nice*?

Heidi asked herself, while tears threatened. Only her pride stopped her from snatching hold of Stefano's arm and demanding that he say something to her.

Into her mind swept Gina's extravagant wedding dress, which Gina had shyly shown her only yesterday. Running a fingertip over its frills and flounces and its satin bodice, Heidi had shamelessly put herself and Stefano into Gina's and her fiancé's places. Did she want that? Did she and Stefano know each other well enough for such a commitment?

'I hear Gina's invited you to her wedding,' Stefano said, and hope flared in Heidi again. If he was thinking of weddings . . . 'We'll see each other then, of course.'

'Of course,' Heidi agreed, lowering her eyes to stare blankly at a row of flowers whose names she had forgotten and whose colors and shapes were blurring with the treacherous pricking of her tears. How could he be so cheerful?

★ ★ ★

'But I'd like to see you much sooner. Every day. I can't stand the thought of not seeing you every day.' Stefano nervously drummed his fingers along the edge of the small marble fountain where he and Heidi had first kissed. Did she remember? Dare he say more about his feelings?

She was determinedly not looking at him. Watching her small, dark-haired figure peering through the fine spray of the fountain, Stefano felt a surge of love punch through his chest and middle. 'Do you know how you've changed all our lives?' he burst out. 'Because of you, I now feel that I truly belong to this family, like a full son.'

She raised her beautiful blue-green eyes, her face haunting in its bewilderment. 'Did you not realize that, Stefano? They chose you.'

Her words gave him a chance that he seized at once. 'As I would choose you, Heidi. I would like there to be more between us than the friendship of family. I would like to visit you in your home town and spend as much time as possible with you, learn everything about you.'

★ ★ ★

'Why?' Heidi asked, feeling for an instant like a gambler, risking everything on a single result. She trembled as Stefano took her in his arms, lowering that bright blond head closer, closer . . .

He kissed her, murmuring endearments in Italian and English, saying that he loved the little gap between her front teeth, that she smelled like wine and roses and honey to him. 'I love you, my Heidi. I love you so much. I want us to be together. I want to learn aromatherapy from you and teach you all I know. I want to show you where I was born. I want to show you the orphanage. I want to come to Selby, where you live. When can I come? When?'

'Soon,' Heidi promised. 'Very soon.' Giddy at the confirmation of Stefano's love, she blushed with pleasure at the thought of finally learning more about him and of his seeing where she lived. 'I love you,' she said simply, feeling herself coloring more deeply at the delicious idea of teaching him, of learning from him.

'Good!' said Stefano, kissing her again. 'I would like you to be thinking of rings, my Heidi. An engagement ring, a wedding ring —'

'You will choose a wedding ring, too?' Heidi asked. 'I'd like that.'

'Of course! I want to show the world that you have chosen me!' Drawing back from her only a little, Stefano wound an arm tenderly about her waist. Listening to the midday bells ringing out again over the city of Bologna, he and Heidi continued their walk past the fountain, along the gravel path bordered with red roses, and so back to the villa, to tell the family their news.

We do hope that you have enjoyed reading this large print book.

Did you know that all of our titles are available for purchase?

We publish a wide range of high quality large print books including:
Romances, Mysteries, Classics
General Fiction
Non Fiction and Westerns

Special interest titles available in large print are:
The Little Oxford Dictionary
Music Book, Song Book
Hymn Book, Service Book

Also available from us courtesy of Oxford University Press:
Young Readers' Dictionary
(large print edition)
Young Readers' Thesaurus
(large print edition)

For further information or a free brochure, please contact us at:
Ulverscroft Large Print Books Ltd.,
The Green, Bradgate Road, Anstey,
Leicester, LE7 7FU, England.
Tel: (00 44) **0116 236 4325**
Fax: (00 44) **0116 234 0205**

OUR LIPS ARE SEALED

Philippa Carey

Francis, Viscount Hilton, has twin stepsisters who are complete hoydens and give him no peace at all. He eventually takes them to London for the season, hoping to find suitably strong-minded husbands to take them off his hands. But he knows nobody in London society and needs the help of their widowed second cousin Jane, Lady Orwell. Francis has no desire to be married himself. Jane has no intention of remarrying either. However, their respective mothers have quite different ideas . . .